CALL O.

CW00505344

A white man 'going native' in the
jungle of Borneo was going to make a
splendid story—and it was newspaper
girl Sara Chesworth's job to get it.
But the white man had views of his
own on the subject, and Sara was
finding her task far from easy. Even
before she complicated matters by
falling in love with him . . .

CALL OF THE HEATHEN

BY

ANNE HAMPSON

MILLS & BOON LIMITED
LONDON W1

First published 1980
Australian copyright 1980
Philippine copyright 1980
This edition 1980

© Anne Hampson 1980

ISBN 0 263 73248 7

Set in Linotype Baskerville 10/10 pt.

Made and printed in Great Britain by
Richard Clay (The Chaucer Press), Ltd., Bungay, Suffolk

CHAPTER ONE

ALTHOUGH at twenty-five Sara Chesworth was one of the
leading journalists on the *Sunday Sphere*, it came as a
complete surprise to her colleagues that she had been
given the assignment which would take her deep into the
primitive jungle of Borneo where, it was rumoured, a
white man had settled with the Natives, adopting their
way of life, living by the blowpipe, dressing in a loincloth, and even taking part in pagan ceremonial.

'He's a sort of Tarzan,' explained Joe, the editor, 'but
he lives with natives, not apes.' His deep-set grey eyes
were fixed upon her face. She had a touching, tender
quality about her looks, a tranquil beauty that seemed
at variance with the toughness of the job she did. Joe,
a happily married man with a super family of two sons
and a daughter, had fallen madly in love with her. But
he was no philanderer; his wife had been true to him
and he meant to be true to her. So when he heard the
rumour about the white man living among the primitive
jungle tribes he had not only been keenly interested in
having a special feature in the colour magazine of his
newspaper, but he had also seen a way of putting this
lovely girl out of his life for a while, hoping that by the
time she returned from what promised to be a fairly long
trip, he would be completely cured. 'I wouldn't give
the job to a woman in the ordinary way,' he continued at
length, 'but you—well, you've proved over and over
again that you can take care of yourself. In any case,' he
added wryly, 'there's this business of the equality of the

sexes; you've as much right to the job as any of the male members of staff.'

Sara had to smile, fully aware of the reason for his sending her away, aware too that the assignment had not been offered to any other member of staff, a circumstance that had caused a measure of discontent among the men, since some of them, being unattached, would have welcomed the opportunity of a trip into the jungle of Borneo. She knew that Joe was in love with her but suspected that he was unaware of her knowledge. She admired his strength of will in deciding to get rid of her for a while. Not that she would have had an affair with him—no hole-and-corner love affair for her! She had ideals which she meant to keep, convinced that some-where in the world was the man of her dreams, a man who would be worth waiting for.

Her eyes went to Joe's face again and she noticed the tightness round his mouth. He was suffering, but he'd get over it. For herself—had he been free she might have let herself care, because she admired and respected him above any other man except her father who, widowed when Sara was nine, had managed to run the house, to care for his daughter and to run a small business. He had married again a year ago and was now living in Scotland, where he was working with an oil company.

Joe was speaking, asking anxiously if she were thinking of changing her mind about the job he wanted her to do.

'You did accept yesterday,' he reminded her.

'Not quite, Joe. I merely said I was interested, that it could prove exciting.' She pushed a hand through soft fair hair, and a tiny sigh escaped her. 'You're so sure I can take care of myself, aren't you?'

'You've done it many times before, Sara.'

'Not in a primitive jungle where you find apes and

snakes and other dangerous creatures, to say nothing of the Natives themselves. That head-hunting business was no joke. They just chopped off heads for sport.' Her eyes, large and brown and widely-spaced, had a faintly anxious look within their depths. 'Since the time when you offered me the job I've been reading up, and there's a pretty grim history attached to the various tribes of Borneo.'

'They were managed very successfully by the White Rajahs, the Brooke rulers, and nowadays one never hears of such things as head-hunting.'

'Not near the coast, but this white man lives in the interior, you said.'

'In the *ulu*—that's far into the centre of the jungle.'

Miles and miles from civilisation, inaccessible in parts. There were no roads—only rivers to travel by. Sara had done her homework well and she was under no illusions regarding the dangers facing her if she agreed to take this trip. True, the Sarawak authorities were providing two guides who were thoroughly trustworthy and who would be with her all the time. They were Dyaks who spoke good English, whose way of life was dramatically different from that of their ferocious grandfathers. They had come down to the coast, brought by their fathers, and were being educated at a college near Kuching, the capital of Sarawak. They were at present on vacation and, like most of the students, were eager to find jobs that would bring them in some money.

'Is anything known of this man's past?' Sara put the question automatically, born of her thoughts. For it had suddenly occurred to her that a man who had elected to abandon the civilised life might be a criminal, an escapee from justice . . . a murderer, perhaps. If so, how was he going to treat a woman journalist whose sole reason for being there was to lay open his secrets, to probe into his affairs with the object of collecting sufficient material for an article in one of Britain's most popular Sunday newspapers?

Joe was shaking his head. Sara noticed the firm contours of his face, the sincere grey eyes. Yes, she could have let herself care. . . . Better to thrust out all hesitations regarding this assignment and get away before she, too, began to suffer heartache.

'That's what's so intriguing,' said Joe. 'Like Tarzan, he could be *somebody*. Who knows? Several well-known men have done the disappearing trick over the past ten years or so.'

'He could be a criminal.'

'Unlikely. His presence there is known—has been since those two geologists I told you about came across him. So if he was a wanted man he'd have been brought in before now.'

She was forced to agree, but before she could say any more the telephone rang and she lapsed into a thoughtful silence while Joe answered it. She supposed there could be a dozen reasons for the white man's presence in the jungle. And that was what her mission was all about; she was to find out who he was, make discoveries regarding his past, find out why he had chosen to live in a steaming jungle rather than his own country. In short, she was to clear up the mystery, then publish her findings.

The two geologists who worked for the Sarawak government had come upon the man accidentally, and he had not seen them at first. They heard him speaking to one of the tribe, first in the native language and then in English. He spoke slowly and distinctly, giving the two men the impression that he was teaching the Native English. When the men revealed themselves, emerging from their place of concealment, the Englishman disappeared with the silence and agility of the jungle-born, and they had never seen him again. None of the Natives would talk about him, or reveal his whereabouts, so the geologists left the interior with the mere knowledge that a white man was living as one of the tribe, an interesting tribe, dynamic, and unquestionably the finest boatmen in the whole country, for the river running through their particular territory was reputed to be the most treacherous in all Borneo, with a number of dangerous rapids which had to be negotiated in order to travel at all. This was done always by *prahu*, a small boat that was handled with incredible skill by the members of this particular tribe which, the geologists said, was called the Ubani Ulu.

Joe replaced the telephone receiver and their eyes met. He smiled, as if wanting to reassure her. His faith in her was such that he had no doubts whatsoever regarding her capability in carrying out the mission with both success, and safety to herself. Her looks were deceptive, with those exquisitely-contoured features, that little retroussé nose with its delicately-arched nostrils. Her lips tilted upwards at each corner and her chin was firmly modelled. This latter was the only real indication of strength in a face of incomparable beauty and proportion.

A little piqued by his confidence—although she could not have explained why—Sara mentioned something else she had read in one of the books about Borneo which she had got from the library.

'The Natives still have skulls hanging up in their longhouses—shrunken heads which they regard as trophies. There were photographs——' She broke off, shuddering. 'They looked like bunches of coconuts,' she added finally.

'They might have the skulls hung up, but they're

ancient ones they don't want to part with. I believe they consider them to be sacred, and do all sorts of things so they won't upset them.'

'They put food near them——' Again she broke off, frowning. She did not want to talk about human skulls any more. 'This man . . . he wears a loincloth, so the geologists said. I don't fancy sitting there, in the middle of the jungle asking questions of a man who's near naked.'

Joe almost scowled at her and she realised he was on the verge of one of those 'awkward' moods which were so familiar to his staff.

'Good lord, Sara, you can't be queasy about a small thing like that! Just look back on some of the jobs you've done since coming to the *Sphere*! What about those two Danes you went looking for in the desert? They'd settled by an oasis and were cultivating the land——'

'There's no comparison,' she broke in, her own temper becoming frayed. 'They were civilised! I imagine that this other's gone back to the savage stage—almost!'

'Those two who saw him said he spoke in a cultured voice—I've already told you that.'

'What has his voice to do with it? The fact that he's gone native proves he's not normal, so he could be dangerous, even more dangerous than the old type of Native.'

Joe drew an exasperated breath.

'He won't rape you, if that's what you're worrying about. He's probably got several wives——' He wagged a knowing forefinger at her. 'When a man's had a Native girl he doesn't ever again have much time for an English one. They're cold and unemotional in comparison.'

'Thanks!' she retorted tartly.

'No offence meant, Sara. I'm just stating facts in an

effort to reassure you.' He paused a moment and she wondered if he were having second thoughts about sending her into the unknown. He was trying to reassure *her*, he said, but there was now a measure of anxiety on his rugged, handsome features. She realised that in spite of what she had been saying she would be bitterly disappointed if he changed his mind and she lost the job to someone else. She had always been adventurous, which was the main reason for her choosing journalism as a career; it promised the unusual, the risky . . . and now, the dangerous. 'Would you like Graham to go with you?' asked Joe at last, and she shook her head instantly. There was keen competition between Graham Findlay and herself and on more than one occasion he had done what she termed his 'swooping' trick and grabbed a story from under her nose. If he went with her the story would be his: Sara was in no doubt about that.

'No,' she said. 'If these two guides are as trustworthy as you've been assured they are, I'll be all right.'

'Good girl! You'll be famous when we produce the story, and the pictures which you always take so well. It'll be the scoop of the year!'

'You're taking a lot for granted, Joe,' she had to remind him. 'This man's not going to fall over me with his story. In fact, I shall have the greatest difficulty in getting him to talk.'

'How can you say that?'

'It's obvious that he guards his privacy. He wasn't having anything to do with those two geologists, was he?' Sara leant back in her chair, crossing her shapely legs and frowning a little as Joe ran his appreciative eyes over her from head to foot.

'But then,' he said quietly at length, 'they weren't you. A man'd have to be made of stone to ignore you.'

Her mouth went tight.

'You've just said that he wouldn't be interested in a cold unemotional Englishwoman!' she almost snapped.

'Don't let's fight,' he said, smiling at her. 'You'll get the story, and lots of photographs.' He paused, but added when she did not speak, 'The end product's going to be worth any small discomforts you might have to put up with.'

Small discomforts! Sara, her feelings mixed, knew for sure that there would be major discomforts, that this was without doubt going to be the toughest job she had tackled in all her years with the *Sphere*. Yet she knew an avid desire to get moving, since the job offered so much in spite of the dangers involved.

She glanced at Joe, but her thoughts had switched wholly to the white man whose private affairs she was hoping to make public for all and sundry to read about. She knew she would be extremely fortunate to get anything much from the man himself, and her main reliance was on the Natives, from whom she hoped to gain most of the information required for a good story. The two guides would translate for her; she was taking an abundance of gifts with which to bribe the Natives— tobacco and cigarettes, lengths of gay printed cloth for sarongs, mirrors and trinkets, and chocolate and sweets for the children. As for the pictures—she would have to get them surreptitiously, but she knew there would be an abundance of places of concealment from where she could put her camera to good use.

It was to be hoped, she suddenly thought with a frown, that the man did not discover what she was about. And all at once the hazards of the jungle faded into nothingness beside the picture of the man's reaction if she should be caught taking a picture. She gave an involuntary shudder and Joe asked lightly what she was thinking about.

'The Wild Man of Borneo,' she said, and saw no reason at all why he should suddenly burst out laughing.

Muda and Tama had both heard of the white man but had never seen him, as it was a long time since they had lived in the jungle. But in any case, they were not of the Ubani Ulu tribe and had never been into their territory, which was in the deepest and densest part of the jungle, their *penghulu*, or chief, living in the longhouse which was at the confluence of the Kalui and Saleh rivers. They were young and strong, spoke English excellently and were eager for the opportunity of some work and also for the opportunity of going into the *ulu*. Sara, who had spent a week at an hotel in Kuching, had got to know the boys and not only liked them but felt fully confident that she would be perfectly safe with them. She was assured by the authorities that the tribes she would meet would be friendly, and that the particular tribe known as the Ubani Ulu, though once the fiercest head-hunters in the country, were now friendly towards visitors, but she must make sure to take plenty of trinkets and other gifts, and must also not do anything to offend them, especially the chief or any of his wives.

The first part of the journey was by a comfortable boat, but later she had to transfer to a *prahu*, which was more fitted to the hazardous travel along narrow streams where *batangs* were often obstacles which had to be removed. These fallen trees would often block the river completely, in which case it took the two men all their time to dispense with them, even having to cut them in two. At other times they merely blocked part of the river and could more easily be pushed to one side.

Another obstacle encountered was the masses of water-weed that clogged up the free passage of the river.

It was a dangerous stream, with rapids formed by hard bands of rock that had survived the merciless battering of the water. Its banks were lined with palisades of nipa palms; behind these were steaming patches of marsh and mangrove swamps, while further back still were the tall jungle trees, dark, mysterious and a little frightening as they spread up the mountainsides. The two youths sang as they steered the *prahu* up the river and Sara was left with her own thoughts. She leant back in her seat, which was in the middle of the boat, and shaded by a palm thatch. Her mind was one moment on the unknown man she was hoping to track down, but the next on the conversation she had had with one of her colleagues, Jack Gordon, whose dark warning on the night he had taken her out to dinner rang in her ears.

'You'll live to regret it, Sara! This is no task for a woman—a trek into the heart of the jungle. You've no protection if you're attacked, either by animals or Natives. And if that wasn't all, there's this mysterious bloke who's gone native. He's unlikely to have seen a white woman in years, so if you do catch up with him you're going to find yourself in a damned dangerous situation!'

'Joe says that a man who's had Native girls never wants an Englishwoman.'

'What the hell does Joe know about it?' he demanded furiously. He had always wanted to be more than a friend to Sara and he made no attempt to disguise the fact that he was anxious about her, had been since the moment he learned of the assignment. 'The man might never have had a Native girl, anyway!'

'Well, if he's a celibate type he won't be interested in

me,' Sara responded logically, but all she heard in response was a snort of impatience, so she swiftly changed the subject, and although he several times tried to reintroduce it she managed to divert him until he was leaving her, dropping her at the door of her flat.

'This head of yours,' he said, giving her gleaming hair a little tug, 'would make a highly coveted trophy, so watch yourself!'

Sara's reverie was broken by Muda leaping overboard to remove a *batang* lying across the stream. As he got aboard again he pointed to a bend in the river.

'We're near a village, miss,' he said, his broad grin revealing several gold teeth. 'We will stop for a little while.'

Sara frowned and said she would rather carry on, but Muda's response was that the *tua rumah*, or headman, would be offended if they went by the longhouse and did not call.

At this Sara gave a resigned shrug and about ten minutes later, on reaching the bend in the river, the boys steered the boat into a small creek along which they proceeded beneath a canopy of intertwined branches and lianas until, after taking another bend, the vista of a meadow spread before Sara's eyes and on this was the *rumah pangai*—or longhouse—its backcloth the deep forest and then the dark mountains whose summits were enveloped in cloud. Soon she was stepping ashore, apprehensively aware that if she missed the narrow path she would sink into the swampy ground.

The *tua rumah* was already coming down the notched tree trunk that served as a ladder to the longhouse, which was built on piles, high above the swamp beneath. Sara was struck by the sort of quiet dignity with which he approached her, extending a hand for her to take. She glanced swiftly over his sarong-clad figure, taking in the intricate tattooing on his arms and chest. He wore beads round his neck, and in his ears ornaments made from the fangs of a clouded leopard. His hair was black and short, with a rounded fringe on his deeply-lined forehead. He spoke some English, enough to greet her and welcome her to the village. He then spoke to Tama, who turned to Sara to say that the headman wanted them to take refreshments. Sara was not very enthusiastic about eating the food, or drinking the rice wine which she had been told about but, afraid of offending the headman, she produced a ready smile and told Tama she would be delighted to have the refreshments offered.

Muda gave her a helping hand to negotiate the long, notched log which gave access to the verandah. On reaching it Sara was subjected to stares from brown women and children who were squatting on rush mats outside their 'doors'. Each door was in reality a dwelling, which was private to the family occupying it, while the verandah was public—like a village street, in fact, for the longhouse was the village, and it could accommodate as many as eighty families. Outside each door was a conglomeration of articles including brass gongs and dragon jars, and an assortment of vases—ancient earthenware pots brought by the Chinese centuries ago. Hanging up were parangs and deer antlers, and skulls covered with human flesh so shrunken and smoked that the skin looked like parchment, black with age. Sara shuddered, wondering why, seeing that head-hunting was no longer the practised sport of these people, they should keep these hideous trophies of a bygone age. How could any white man live with people like these? she wondered, fascinated by all she saw. Beneath the floor of the verandah—which was slatted—were the long-

nosed pigs and the poultry. The smell drifted up,
nauseating but bearable. She was invited to sit down on
a mat, was given rice biscuits to eat and *tuak* to drink.
She later gave the headman some cigarettes and a length
of cotton cloth for a sarong. He thanked her gravely, and
accompanied her down the ladder. Just before saying
goodbye she asked Tama to enquire about the white
man, which he did, and Sara saw the face of the *tua ramah*
close, and the half-smile wiped instantly from it.

'Sulan Dalan will not talk of the white man,' she was
told by Tama. 'But I can tell that he knows about him.'

'I see. . . .' Sara's eyes went to the headman again; he
moved a hand, indicating the *prahu*. She had overstayed
her welcome, obviously.

She said goodbye again and turned, treading the
uneven ground carefully as before, keeping to the
narrow path made by the Natives.

It was forty-eight hours later that Muda told her they
would be in Ubani Ulu territory very soon. She had
spent the previous night in a tent set up for her on an
island in the middle of the river through which they had
been travelling. It was wider than most of the others
they had come up, and the island had been formed by
the braiding of the stream many years before. Darkness
had descended rapidly; the night was cool after the
torrid heat of the afternoon, and Sara reclined on a mat
outside the tent, enveloped by a delicious sense of ease
under a million stars. She slept soundly and awoke to a
glorious dawn where fire topped the mountains and
spread, like molten lava, down through the jungle and
on to the water of the stream.

'How long shall we be in getting there?' She found, as
she asked Tama the question, that her heart was hammer-

ing and her pulses were not normal either.

'By this afternoon we shall be there, miss.'

Only a few hours. . . . Would she come face to face with the man right away, or would he be as elusive to her as he had been with the two geologists? Even if she were successful in making contact there was no knowing how he would treat her. He could turn nasty, in which case she might find herself being treated 'rough'. For it was not to be supposed that he would care one jot for chivalry. Living as he did with pagans, he would have forgotten about such things a long while ago. Women to him would now be regarded as mere chattels born and reared for man's pleasure, his slave and possession. What would he care for an Englishwoman's feelings, or her ideas of equality?

'We'll be able to camp all right?'

The Dyak boy nodded his head.

'We can camp if you like, miss, but also we shall be invited to stay in the *rumah pengai*.'

'I don't want to stay in the longhouse, Tama. I'd prefer to camp.' She was thinking that the white man would be living in the longhouse, and she was not at all keen on being that close, having him watch all she was doing.

Tama said nothing and she fell silent again, becoming immersed in her own thoughts. But part of her mind was inevitably on her surroundings. The dense tangled jungle on either side was primary jungle, probably untouched by man since the beginnings of time. Noble trees towered over the river, and the dark primeval arbours were a playground for monkeys who leapt and scampered through the foliage, chattering unceasingly.

Muda was as much in the water as in the boat, as the tangled masses of water-weed blocked the narrow river incessantly and had to be removed. But he seemed to enjoy it all, because there was always a broad smile on his brown face when he leapt into the *prahu* again. It was an upstream journey, with the impression of remoteness growing all the time. The mountains were sullen, their peaks lost in low and threatening clouds, but from this hidden watershed a labyrinth of streams and channels meandered down, to pass through the mangrove swamps on their way to the river and its tributaries. The river was narrowing even more now and the trees, dripping wet, met overhead. In these trees hung a maze of parasitic plants, reaching for the light, and the ground between the swamps was laced with tangled roots. Fallen and decaying trees, masses of floating leaves, the cry of a gibbon, the fleeting impression of a Yellow-Crowned Bulbul flitting about in the overhanging boughs. . . . All these lent atmosphere and seemed for some indefinable reason to bring Sara's position right home to her, and to send feathery ripples along her spine, the prescience of danger. . . .

CHAPTER TWO

MUDA brought the *prahu* to the bank and within less than three minutes Sara was staring up into the thin, wizened face of the village headman. Tama had introduced her to him and said she was looking for the white man who was supposed to be living with the tribe. The *tua rumah*'s mouth had gone thin, his eyes had narrowed. Sara's heart sank even before Tama said,

'He will not speak to you of the white man, miss. He

says that we must leave his village and not come back.'

'Can't you bribe him?' said Sara desperately. 'Tell him
I have tobacco and whisky and——'

'I have said this——' Tama shrugged his shoulders.
'He says we must leave.'

She gave a deep sigh and turned resignedly.

'There is another longhouse farther up-river, you said?'

'There is,' answered Tama, following as she went back
to the bank where the *prahu* was lying. 'You want to go
there?'

'Yes, Tama, I must keep on trying. . . .' Her voice
trailed off to silence and her eyes widened to their full
extent. Coming down the notched ladder from the longhouse was a tall, lithe-framed man in a loin-cloth, his
body the colour of matured teak, his hair—dark and
sprinkled with grey at the temples—reaching to his
gleaming, naked shoulders. He was barefooted and from
a distance could have been taken for one of the Natives
who were standing about, staring curiously at the white
woman who had come into their midst. But he was no
Native, this man with the noble bearing, whose unhurried
movements, even, spelt distinction. The outdoor life had
carved his features as the elements of wind and water
carve the face of a rock. His dark skin was weather-
toughened, his eyes shrewd and penetrating. He pos-
sessed an unassailable air of dignity and superiority that
amounted to nothing less than arrogance. Her eyes met
his, and instantaneous upon it a fluttering sensation
touched her nerves.

'You. . . .' She had never rehearsed what she would
say when she met the man—*if* she met him. And now
she was at a complete loss, too taken aback by his
unexpected appearance to be able to collect her thoughts,

much less find words to suit the occasion. 'You're the—the white man.'

'You are looking for me?' The voice, though cultured and quiet, had a harsh edge to it which seemed to match the fine-drawn intentness of his eyes as they subjected her to an unswerving, sphinx-like stare. He seemed not only to be taking her measure, but absorbing every single thing about her face—her mouth and eyes, the shade and texture of her skin. The grey eyes moved slowly over her figure, stripping every shred of clothing from her body. Confusion brought colour to her face, much to her chagrin. What had happened to the cool assurance which seven years with the newspaper had given her? It seemed to have deserted her altogether, erased by a feeling of inferiority, of total inadequacy, for this man was disconcerting, to say the very least. The pose, the stillness, that riveted stare. The entire aura around him savoured of the grotesque, of heathenism. Sara swallowed convulsively, searching for words. She saw his mouth compress and realised he was waiting, impatiently, for her answer.

'Yes—er—I was looking for—for you.'

The grey eyes narrowed to mere slits. But before he had time to speak a roll of thunder was heard overhead, and a few spots of rain warned of the tropical storm to come. All the men glanced skywards, and as Sara herself looked up she glimpsed brown faces on the verandah of the longhouse, the curious, interested faces of the women and children of the village.

'You'd better come inside and shelter.' Abrupt the invitation, which had scarcely been uttered when the raindrops became as large as marbles. Equatorial storms came suddenly and often died just as suddenly, with the sun appearing immediately afterwards, and drying everything up again.

'Thank you.' She turned as she began to follow him, looking for her two bodyguards.

'They'll find their own shelter,' snapped the Englishman. 'Come along!' It was an order, rapped out in hard, abrupt tones which brought two bright little spots of colour to Sara's cheeks. However, she obeyed, telling herself that there might be a chance of learning something about the man. He passed several doors before turning into one. She followed and he closed the door behind her. 'Sit down!' He threw a hand carelessly towards a rough truckle bed which was covered with a brightly-coloured blanket. The only other items of furniture in the apartment were a table, two chairs and a cupboard of sorts in the corner behind the door. A rush mat covered part of the floor, which was of wooden planks which had been roughly placed together, so roughly that there were gaps between them through which daylight could be seen—and through which came the pungent odour of pigs and poultry.

She perched herself right on the edge of the bed and then wished she hadn't, because the man was standing, well over six feet in height, close to her, staring down with hard arrogant eyes.

'Who are you?' he demanded. 'And how do you come to be looking for me?'

She hesitated, debating an answer. But she soon realised that there was no subtle way of handling this situation and she said, having regained some degree of composure,

'I'm a journalist and——'

'A *journalist*!' He spat out the word, his eyes mere slits in a face that had blackened with fury. 'And what the hell has a journalist to do with me?' His glance roved her body, insolence in its depths . . . and something else which she did not like at all, for again she was stripped, and thoroughly examined. 'Where are you from?'

'London—the *Sunday Sphere*. I—we heard about you from two geologists——'

'And you thought it would make a good scoop, eh?' His eyes smouldered, like white-hot ash about to ignite. She noticed the snarl-like twist of his lips, the rigid pose of the aquiline features, and an involuntary shiver passed through her.

'It's an unusual story, Mr——?'

A sneer caught his lips, forming the hint of a smile.

'Nothing doing!' he said. 'Here, I'm known as Linjau.'

She repeated it, then asked if it had any special meaning. He paused a moment as if debating whether or not to answer.

'It means—tiger,' he said at length.

Sara looked at him doubtfully. He shrugged his shoulders as if to tell her that he didn't give a damn whether she believed it or not.

He walked over to a sort of shutter made of plaited palm leaves and lifted it up to reveal an aperture underneath. Sara had a glimpse of the jungle outside and then the storm broke and the rain lashed down in torrents to the accompaniment of thunder and lightning.

'You must have been crazy to come out here, expecting to get a story.' He turned around, the sneer back on his lips. 'Did no one tell you of the dangers of the jungle?'

'I knew of them,' she answered quietly. 'I've had tough assignments before, and managed them successfully.'

'You won't manage this successfully,' he assured her.

'There's a chance you'll get back safely, but no chance that you'll get a story.'

She looked at him, at the compression of the thin lips above a determined, outthrust chin, at the hollows beneath the high prominent cheekbones. She let her eyes move to the near-naked body, taking a fleeting survey before, embarrassed, she glanced down. The strength! It was there, hidden beneath the dark leanness of his frame.

She said, feeling the necessity to break the silence that was between them,

'I don't know how any white man could forsake the civilised life for one like this——' She spread a hand deprecatingly. 'It's—awful!'

The grey, metallic eyes glinted.

'You are not getting a story,' he repeated, 'so you can keep all the tricks of the trade for another time and place!'

She flushed, her teeth snapping together. She would get a story if it was the last thing she did!

'I think the rain is stopping,' she said frigidly, 'so I'll be on my way.'

He stared at her for a long moment and then,

'Where are you going?'

'That,' she said tautly, 'is my business.'

'On the other hand, it might be mine.'

'What do you mean?'

'If I hear of you going to other villages, snooping around, bribing the Natives with liquor and tobacco, I'll deal with you in a way that'll not only prove effective in this particular case, but that will put you out of business for some considerable time to come.' No roughness in the voice now. On the contrary, it was almost gentle . . . dangerously gentle. . . . Sara felt the chill of real fear creeping along her spine and she shivered involuntarily. Nevertheless, she was not going to allow this hateful creature, this heathen, to intimidate her, or to let him see that she was in any way affected by his threat.

'I intend to carry out my task to the best of my ability,' she told him forcefully. 'I've been sent out here at a great expense to my employers and they've every right to expect something for their money.'

He came close, his bare feet noiseless on the floor.

'Are you telling me that despite what I've said you're still going to try and get a story?'

'Your threats don't deter me. I've met people before who are obstinate——' She stopped abruptly, wishing she could take back those words, for they were certainly not what she should have voiced.

'Obstinate?' he repeated harshly. 'So because I want my life to be private, my secrets to remain my own—I'm obstinate? Young woman, take care!' He wagged a lean and threatening finger close to her face. 'You're in hostile territory, and if you're wise you will keep that firmly in your mind!' He went to the door and flung it open. 'Get out!' he snarled, 'and remember my warning!'

She went, her heart beating overrate. She negotiated the long notched ladder carefully, making use of the frail handrail, and was glad when she reached the bottom. Her feet sank into the ground, which was sodden after the rain. She glanced up; he was there on the verandah, with several women and children crowding close, looking down at her. She turned away, saw that Tama and Muda were in the *prahu*, and went as swiftly as the precarious ground would allow, relieved to get into the boat yet at the same time feeling frustrated at not being able to glean any information at all. But she was still eager for a story; the man intrigued her more than ever now that she had met him, as she was sure he was no ordinary person, that his background had been cultured and aristocratic. Why had he come here in the first place and, more important, what had decided him to stay? Was he intending to live here for the rest of his days? Was he married? Did he have children . . . little brown ones who would be brought up pagans? So many questions, and Sara set her mouth. She was determined to find out something about him!

It was a mere three hours later that they reached another longhouse, belonging to the same tribe, the Ubani Ulu, and this time she was rather more fortunate. She distributed cigarettes and whisky as largesse the moment she arrived, and received eager smiles all around. A length of bright cotton cloth was given to one of the *tua rumah*'s wives and another to his daughter. Tama and Muda meanwhile were speaking to some of the Natives who had crowded together on the river bank close to where the *prahu* was moored and as she glanced at them Muda made the thumbs-up sign and her spirits lifted. One of the Natives, Agan—who had received gifts from her—was willing to talk.

When she came away an hour or so later she was in possession of several interesting facts about the white man. He had come to the island originally to spend a month's holiday with a friend who was manager of an oil company in Brunei, and the two made a trip into the interior of the jungle. The visitor seemed deeply impressed by the simplicity of the Native way of life, and went again, on his own, into the *ulu* before going home to England. In his absence something serious had apparently happened, because he returned to his friend looking years older than he had before.

'Agan worked for the oil company at that time as a labourer,' Tama said, 'but he did not know what had happened to the white man. He was looking very unhappy and he had gone grey at the sides of his head.'

'It sounds as if some tragedy had occurred while he was here, in Borneo,' put in Sara thoughtfully. She and the two Dyak boys were in the *prahu* and she was sitting in the middle of it, sheltered as usual by the palm thatch above her head. She was taking notes as Tama related what he had been told by Agan. 'The white man's friend called him John,' continued Tama, 'but Agan does not know his other name.' He went on to say that this John's friend was moved to South America but John stayed in Borneo. He could not live in the compound where he had stayed with his friend because the house belonged to the oil company.

'He moved from there, Agan said, and went into the *ulu*, living with one tribe and then another.' Tama paused to give Sara time to make her notes. When she had finished Sara remarked thoughtfully,

'He must have paid for his keep, surely?'

Muda broke in at this point to say that the man always seemed to have plenty of money when he was staying with his friend.

'Agan said he was a wealthy man in his own country,' added Muda finally, and then went on with the business of steering the boat round a fallen tree that lay in the river but to one side of it.

'Agan told the white man about his tribe, the Ubani Ulu, and he decided to go there. Agan went back himself a little while later because he did not like living away from the *ulu*.'

'He couldn't settle? Not like you, Tama?'

The boy grinned, showing his gold teeth.

'No, not like me. I came down to the coast when I was young, you see. I think it is not easy when you are older and have been brought up in the jungle.'

Sara nodded, but thought of the man who had found no difficulty in doing it the other way round, exchanging the civilised life for that of the jungle.

'This John settled with the Ubani Ulu then? How long has he been with them?'

'Agan thinks about six or seven years——' He stopped to grin ruefully. 'They do not trouble about time in this part of the world.'

How marvellous not to be ruled by time! Not to know how old you were. . . .

'Has he always lived in the same place—in that apartment he took me to?'

'No, that is not where he lives. He has a hut near the village where the *penghulu* lives. He is a friend of the big chief.'

'What was he doing there, then?' enquired Sara, puzzled.

'He was visiting, and they gave him that room.'

'Where is the village of the *penghulu*?'

'Even deeper in the jungle, miss.'

'We will go there, Tama,' she returned decisively. 'It's too late now to make the journey, so we shall camp when you come to a suitable place.' They had been travelling downstream; tomorrow morning they would turn around and travel upstream, going deeper and deeper into the primitive Bornean jungle. She did not care to dwell on another meeting with the man, but she was determined to have one.

CHAPTER THREE

SARA crouched within the shelter of the dense scrub, her camera at the ready. The man calling himself Linjau was standing there, watching women washing clothes in the river, their hands tattooed in a way that made them look as if they were encased in mittens. Heavy earrings had drawn down their ears so that they reached their shoulders. It was a fascinating study, with the man, clad only in a *chawat*, and with his teak-brown body gleaming as if it were coated with oil, looking idly on, and appearing so very like a true Native while at the same time retaining that aura of distinction and nobility. Sara, her breath held and every nerve sharpened, focused carefully, making sure she had the full figure of the man in his loincloth framed in the viewfinder. And then—click! The picture was taken and she relaxed again, letting out her breath slowly.

Then suddenly she was aware that the man's attention had been arrested, that his keen ears and eyes were primitively alert. She stood rooted to the spot, holding her breath again, conscious that she was trembling from head to foot. It seemed an eternity before the man moved, and yet it could have been no more than a few seconds. He leapt like a jungle beast, crashing through the thicket, a curse on his lips. Sara, galvanised into life by the sound rather than the movement, turned to run, scrambling blindly through the oozy soil, making her way through masses and masses of alocasias and anthuriums in an attempt to outpace the man. Alas for her hopes! She ought to have known that anyone as used to the jungle as he would be upon her almost before she knew it. It was her hair that he caught, jerking ruthlessly, forcing her to come to an instant stop, a cry of pain escaping her.

'You bitch!' he snarled, giving her hair another savage tug. 'You snooping, prying bitch!' Before she knew what he was intending the camera was snatched from her hands and with a swing of his wrist it went flying through the air to land in the swamp some distance from where they were standing. Sara put up a trembling hand to her head, sheer fury possessing her at the idea of his hurting her in the way he had, for her head was throbbing with pain that was swiftly spreading from the back to the front and into her eyes. 'How many pictures have you taken?' he demanded. 'I'll have you prosecuted if you dare to publish any!'

'That—that was the—the first,' she quivered, making a move to retrieve her camera. He was before her, his bare feet squelching through the mud. Picking up the camera, he walked to the river's edge and threw it into the stream. The women, having ceased their washing, stared, wide-eyed, as it sank.

'You had no right to destroy my camera!' Sara glowered at him. 'That was a very valuable piece of equipment!'

'Have you any more?'

'Cameras, you mean? Yes, of course——' She stopped, furious with herself for the admission. 'But you won't get your hands on them!' she flashed.

'Don't use them,' he advised. The harsh savagery was gone from his voice. He was weighing her up with arrogant, supercilious attention. That expression again! He was impudently stripping her just as he had done before. 'If you know what's good for you you'll clear out of here while you're in one piece!'

'I'm not expecting to have my head chopped off!' she threw back at him. They were standing on the grass by the river, and the women were chattering excitedly among themselves. Sara would have given a month's salary to know what they were saying. 'I see no reason why I shouldn't remain in one piece!'

The grey metallic eyes narrowed to mere slits.

'Take my advice, woman, and get out of here.'

She glanced around, looking for her two guides, but they were nowhere to be seen. She had told them to keep out of the way while she was taking pictures, but to remain close, just in case she needed their help.

'I shall go when I've done what I came to do,' she managed at length, looking up at him with what she hoped was a fearless expression. 'I'm not going back without some kind of a story.' She knew that was not the thing to say, but the man had infuriated her by savagely tugging at her hair like that and she knew an irrepressible urge to retaliate in any way that presented itself. 'Failure is something I'm not used to!'

'And being spied on is something I'm not used to. If you don't leave this territory immediately I shall have you taken prisoner—and your two bodyguards.'

She blinked at him disbelievingly. But there was that in his expression that convinced her he was in deadly earnest.

'The Sarawak authorities know I've come up here,' she said, but not in the same firm voice as before.

'Many travellers have come up here . . . and never returned. There are many ways one can meet death—a bite from a cobra, for instance.'

She shivered visibly and saw the thin mouth twist in a sort of satisfied smile.

'If—if you were to have me taken a prisoner what would happen?'

'To you? The men might find amusement . . . I might myself,' he added slowly, his eyes roving, finding the tender curves of her breasts, the slender waist, the boyish outline of the hips. She coloured hotly and was amazed to hear him laugh. 'It's a long time since I had the pleasure of making love to a white woman——'

'Shut up!' she broke in wrathfully. 'I'm not going to listen to insults from a man like you!'

'Like me?' he echoed softly. 'And what exactly do you mean by that?'

She turned away, intending to leave him, but she was gripped by the shoulder and wrenched about so that she faced him.

'I asked you a question,' he thundered. 'Answer it!'

Fury equal to his encompassed her whole being.

'You're a drop-out!' she flashed, driven by provocation. 'You're obviously shirking something, refusing to face up to whatever it is you ran away from!' She twisted free and ran, stumbling in the mud, or when her feet came up against tufts of spiky grass. But she reached the *prahu* safely and got aboard. Tama and Muda were not far behind.

'You got your picture, but the man took your camera.' Tama spoke diffidently, as if he had to say something but was at the same time afraid of offending her.

'You saw what happened, then?'

'Yes, miss. We were sorry.'

'Why didn't you come to my assistance?'

Tama said that they did not know what to do. They were afraid when they saw the white man in such a temper, and even more so when he threatened to have them all taken prisoners.

Sara gave an exasperated sigh. A lot of good they were! And yet the next moment she was in a more reasonable frame of mind, admitting that her quarrel with the white man was nothing to do with the two boys, and that they would be jeopardising their chances of employment as guides if they were to become involved in someone else's differences. She was also admitting that the white man had every right to resent what she was trying to do. He wanted privacy; she was endeavouring to intrude into it, and not only that, but she intended to make her findings public. It was wrong. But she was a journalist and her job was to get a good story for her paper. Joe had faith in her ability to do so. She had been sent here at a great expense and something was expected of her in return.

She sat in the boat and argued these points with herself. And although she had no intention of giving up merely because she had lost one of her cameras, she was acutely conscious of the uneasy admission at the back of her mind that neither she nor anyone else had any right to probe and pry into the man's private life.

She drew out her notebook and read what she had previously written about the man. It seemed fairly certain that his reason for being here was that a tragedy of some kind had occurred, either while he was away from home the first time, or soon after he got back.

A tragedy. . . . And she had called him a drop-out, a shirker. She bit her lip till it hurt, filled with self-abasement because of those words she had spoken in anger.

'I ought to go home and leave him alone,' she whispered, 'and yet he intrigues me. I want to know more about him. . . .' And it was not only because of the story, she realised. She wanted to know more about him for some other reason, but what that reason was she could not understand, no matter how hard she tried.

*

She spent the night in the tent which the two boys had rigged up for her beneath a ceiling of intertwined branches and parasitic plants. She had watched the sickle of a young moon swaying between the boughs, had heard the fruit bats, had been startled by cicadas as big as sparrows flying into the tent and crashing into the pressure lantern. And now she had been awakened by the yodel-like *wak-wak-wak* of a gibbon monkey and the song of the bulbuls in the plantains and sago palms. She got up and washed in a bowl of water fetched for her by Muda, from the stream. All around her was lost in a sort of tranquil peace and she felt, deeply, the solitude of the jungle, aware that so much of it was unexplored by man.

The boys had caught a mouse-deer and were cooking its brains in bamboo. Sara shuddered when they offered her some, and had instead a couple of pieces of packet toast and some marmalade. There was coffee, made on a spirit stove, and when she had finished she told the boys to follow her and keep her always in sight.

'You are going again to take pictures of the white man?' asked Muda with a frown of doubt on his dark forehead.

'I shall have another try,' was all she said before moving away, towards the hut where the white man lived. It was made of wood, but very different from the long-house where the *penghulu* lived. Sara had found it yesterday, a few hours after her disastrous encounter with the man who owned it. It had been pointed out to her by Muda, who had been talking to one of the Natives, and to whom he had given a packet of cigarettes passed to him by Sara.

Linjau, the Native told Muda, was gone to the forest to hunt wild pig. She had gone close to the hut and peered in through a gap in the shutters, noticing rattan furniture, matting rugs, a tape-recorder—obviously worked by batteries—two Chinese jade figures standing on a shelf fixed to the wall, a most attractive Ming plaque, and a couple of paintings framed in Thai silk. There was a trestle bed with a hand-woven blanket and, to one side of it, a door leading to what Sara suspected was a kitchen of sorts.

She had pondered over the tape-recorder and wondered if Linjau traded jungle produce—like mouse-deer and pig—for things like batteries and tapes. She would have liked to take pictures of the interior, but of course this was impossible and she had to be satisfied with a photograph of the outside. And today she wanted to get one of the man himself, standing close to his hut, if that were at all possible.

Having learnt from her previous encounter with him she decided on a longer-range shot, and in readiness for this she circled the hut and stayed some way from it, sure that she was completely hidden by the tangled vegetation that was spread around her. It was exciting! To be here, in this jungle, waiting for the man to appear. The shot promised to be one of the finest she had ever taken!

She had not long to wait, and her nerves fairly jerked with excitement when she saw him with a blowpipe, a splendid specimen of manhood in his *chawat*, his skin, as before, gleaming like teak freshly treated with oil. She was at the ready with her camera, but he moved swiftly and she found herself following automatically, treading warily, very conscious of the fact that her foot on a rotten twig would spell disaster even more severe than yesterday. She managed to keep up with him, he in the open and she in the dense protection of the thicket. She was fascinated by the sight of him; he moved with the phantom stealth of nature, his lean body erect, the blow-pipe in his hand, and around his waist a sort of belt carrying a cylinder in which was contained the poison darts, made from the juice of the ipoh tree.

The moments passed, with no real opportunity for a picture, as he was now moving in cover, going through the jungle more silently than a leopard, leaving no trace—no flattened leaves or trodden grass. Sara missed him now and then, but kept catching a glimpse of him, of the broad outline of his gleaming shoulders. There was a calm unhurried efficiency in his stealth, a primitive determination in every step he took. Suddenly she saw his body stiffen and, her heart pounding, she thought for one terrified moment that he had sensed her presence, but it was his quarry he had sighted and she found herself quivering from head to foot at the idea of getting a photograph of him using the blowpipe. She watched him lift it, and point it, his eyes narrowed, his lips slightly pursed. She focused him and took the shot at the same time that he sent the poison dart at his quarry, a long-snouted wild pig which gave just one squeal and then silence. The man had not seen her, so intent was he on his kill. Sara backed away, desiring another shot more than anything but deterred from taking one by the con-viction that she ought not to try her luck any more for the present.

And then, suddenly, she knew she should hide the camera! For the man had swung around when he had covered only half the distance to the pig, and she sensed rather than saw his keen, jungle alertness. Swiftly she tucked the camera away beneath some bushes, and straightened up, to stand irresolute for a space before deciding to come 'out into the open. The man's eyes narrowed, subjecting her to an arrogant, unveiled

CALL OF THE HEATHEN

examination. She watched his expression intently, breathing a sigh of relief when at last she was able to decide that he had not seen the camera.

'What the devil are you doing here?' The voice was like a rasp scraping on her nerve-ends. 'Snooping again—prying into what doesn't concern you!'

Her chin lifted, but the retort that leapt to her lips was stemmed. She felt guilty, half hating herself for the photograph she had taken of him, catching him unawares like that.

'It isn't private property,' she said. 'I'm—er—interested in the jungle.' A lame rejoinder, and she was not in the least surprised when a sneer twisted those thin and arrogant lips of his.

'But more interested in the people who live here, especially one particular person.' His eyes raked her contemptuously and then he turned and went towards the animal he had killed, so swiftly, so humanely. She asked, diverted,

'Will you eat that?'

He was holding it by its back legs, examining it, turning it as he did so.

'How long are you staying here?' he enquired, and she coloured at the snub he had so effectively given her in bypassing her question.

'Until I've got what I want,' she flashed, wishing he would not rile her like this. It made her feel guilty in answering him back in a manner that was so uncivil.

'I've warned you,' he said, coming close, the pig dangling by his side, 'that I'll have you taken prisoner.'

'I've been thinking about your threat, and I'm not at all sure you have the power to have me taken prisoner by the Natives. They're noted for their friendliness to strangers; I was told that when I was in Kuching. You might be interested to know,' she added with a hint of triumph in her voice, 'that the *penghulu* has invited me to a party in the longhouse this evening.'

The grey eyes glittered, flecked with ice. Plainly he was not pleased by the news she had given to him. Nevertheless, there was no animosity in his tone as he explained that it was customary to give a party when a visitor came to the village.

'Had I spoken to him first, though,' he added in a crisper voice, 'he'd probably have sent you packing.'

'You're very sure of your influence with the chief!'

'He's a good friend of mine.' His body jerked, gleaming in the sun. The movement seemed to be a little spasm of irritation, felt against himself, because he was bothering to converse with her.

But she wanted to talk, to stay with him . . . and she knew the desire was not born of the wish for a story, but of something else altogether . . . something indefinable, but important. She said curiously,

'You've been here a long time, Mr—I mean, Linjau ——' She stopped again; it seemed so strange to say the name by which he was known here. 'Can I call you that?' Why she put the question she did not know, but there was so much about herself and her reactions to this man's presence that she did not understand. He drew her in some strange way and she began to wonder if she was becoming attracted to him as a man, because he was different from any other man she had ever known . . . because he had gone primitive . . . pagan. . . .

'Please yourself,' was his surprising reply, spoken with a little less hostility than she expected. 'If we're to be guests of the *penghulu* we shall have to speak—unfortunately.'

Sara felt a hint of colour tinge her cheeks. But she

managed to retain her composure and her reserve as she
rejoined,

'Is it imperative that we speak?'

He nodded absently, his eyes on the animal in his hand.
Behind him the forest trees rose against the hills, and in
them monkeys skipped about, some carrying babies
against their chests.

'It would be an insult to the chief if two of his guests
were unsociable to one another.' A frown came with the
words; he glowered at her, but yet his eyes roved, over
every line and curve of her body. The cotton dress she
wore was fairly short, and it fitted snugly against her
curves, accentuating the outline of their shape. His
attention remained fixed; she coloured hotly and for the
first time saw real amusement on his face. It transformed
him! She caught her breath, trying desperately to throw
off the rising attraction within her. He was *something* and
no mistake! A man apart and above all others—a *he*-man
if ever there was one!

She just had to say, because the silence was unbearable,

'Then we must not offend him, must we?'

'On the contrary, we must please him.' Quiet the
words; she started visibly, nerves alert.

'In wh-what way?' she stammered, and the man
threw back his head and laughed, surprising her even yet
again, and revealing yet again just how attractive he
could be.

'He'll probably expect us to sleep together,' returned
Linjau, the grey eyes glimmering with humour. 'And as
you so rightly say, we must not offend him. When a
female is offered to a male guest in a longhouse the
parties are expected to accept the gesture as a compliment, an honour——'

Sara cut his words short by exclaiming,

'Don't be so absurd! I know of the custom, as it happens! I'm not a fool! I read a bit before coming here. When the chief offers a woman it's one of his wives or daughters!' He was smiling humorously and she glared at him. 'The chief certainly wouldn't offer a white woman simply because she would *not* accept!'

The man lifted his brows a fraction.

'She wouldn't?' He was shaking his head and the smile upon his face became a twisted sneer of contempt. 'What are you trying to do—place your sex on a pedestal? Save your breath. It would run out long before I was convinced!'

The cynicism! She instantly thought of the 'tragedy' which she had supposed had happened in his absence from England. But was it a tragedy . . . or something else? Had some woman let him down? Sara became convinced that at some time in his life he had been let down, but of course she could not reach any conclusions about its occurrence coinciding with his first visit to Borneo to see his friend.

She racked her brain for some retort, but when at last words leapt to her lips they were replaced by a cry as, glancing down, she noticed a leech fastened to her leg just above the knee.

'Oh . . . how revolting!' She had known of these repulsive, avid creatures lurking in the undergrowth, ready to fasten their lips to the skin and suck copious blood, but had not up till now been troubled by them.

'Don't try to pull it off!' The voice came as a snapped command which brought Sara upright again. 'If you do you'll leave the head and have a festering sore that'll give you a great deal of trouble.' He dropped the pig on to the ground and sought a small pouch which was on his belt along with the cylinder holding the poison darts. Sara

watched him take out a cigarette and light it. And then
he told her to pull up her dress, which she did, not
looking at his face. The lighted cigarette did its work;
the leech fell to the ground. Sara felt a trifle sick at the
thought of the creature sucking her blood.

'How did it get there?' she asked. 'After all, I'm not
in any long grass.'

'It probably dropped from a tree,' he returned casually.
'They can smell blood through a person's clothing. On
the other hand, leeches have a light touch, so it could
have been there for some time and you didn't know.
You're lucky it wasn't a dozen.'

'How awful!' She shuddered and heard him say, an
odd inflection in his voice,

'This is no place for a white woman. What the hell
made you come?' He was looking down at her, the
lighted cigarette still in his fingers. She glanced at it, and
at the long lean hand that held it. She had felt the touch
of his hand, fleetingly, as he dealt with the hideous
creature that had attacked her . . . felt the touch and
had quivered in a strange unfathomable way.

'You know why I came,' she murmured. 'It was to try
and get a story.'

'The prospect of glory, too?' His brows lifted, a
gesture of admonishment which caused Sara to advert her
head. 'It would have been a scoop. How disappointing
for you! Do you suppose you're the first who's come here
with the intention of tearing my privacy to shreds merely
for profit and praise?'

'There have been others, then?'

'Several. One died here of a fever and another got in
the way of a king cobra. The others escaped with whole
skins but no stories.' His gaze met hers, but she soon
lowered her eyes again under the burning contempt in

his. 'My life story is not for selling to sensationalists in search of escape from their self-inflicted boredom!' He paused, giving her the chance to speak, but she had nothing to say. He was making her feel like a worm even before he added that people like her ought to be whipped. 'You'll get no story,' he assured her finally, 'so you might as well get back where you belong—and where you're safe.'

CHAPTER FOUR

SARA squatted on a mat made of woven grasses and ate *umai*—slices of raw fish that had been dipped in a special sauce. Linjau was beside her, given the place by Penghulu Miri because, quite naturally, he thought that the two white people would like to be together. There were about thirty families living in the longhouse and they were all there, on the verandah, squatting on rush mats, the men smoking and talking, the women silent, smoking cheroots or chewing betel nuts. They wore brightly-coloured sarongs, with beautiful beads adorning their naked chests. Many wore heavy earrings, and the ears had been so stretched that these earrings were resting on the women's breasts. Linjau, noticing her interest, surprised Sara by explaining just how the holes in the ears came to be so long:

'They begin with one or two rings,' he said, 'and these elongate the ear lobes. Another ring is added, then another and all the time the lobe is being lengthened. They have to be very careful after a while because it's considered a crime if the lobe breaks—all the woman's beauty is gone.'

'So many strange customs,' she murmured, taking a sip of the potent *borak*, the rice wine always offered to visitors and which must never be refused, for to do so would be an insult to the host.

Sara glanced around, taking in the objects that adorned the walls and floor and ceiling. Half a dozen pressure lamps provided illumination and these were placed at intervals along the side of the verandah. On the walls were dangerous-looking parangs and other hunting implements; there was a painted war shield whose thick layer of dust was in keeping with that on the grinning, toothless skulls that hung from deer antlers; there were brass gongs and drums, huge dragon jars and a miscellany of other objects, all valuable and held in esteem, having been handed down from generation to generation and having a superstitious significance as well, for they were, according to their owners, able to bring good luck if treated with respect.

The chief, Penghulu Mira, was dressed for the occasion, with a new sarong made from material which Sara had given him, a plumed cap on his head and heavy earrings in brass. Round his neck he wore an oyster shell and on his arms he had several bangles. Linjau was in shorts and a white shirt which had once had long sleeves, but these had been cut off and, with constant washing, the edges had frayed to a depth of half an inch or more. The shorts were of khaki drill, very old and frayed but obviously newly washed. His hair shone and he was clean-shaven, like the Natives.

The party had begun only a few minutes ago when Penghulu Miri had held a cock bird over the heads of his two guests and spoken friendly words of welcome in the Malay language, a tongue spoken by many of the Natives. Linjau translated these words for Sara's benefit and she thanked him graciously, adding a few words which she wanted him to say to the chief. Smiles all around and then the *borak* was passed round, brought by lovely slender girls, some brown, some buff-coloured but all young and exceedingly attractive. One, Luli, seemed on familiar terms with Linjau, for she hovered over him, making play with her beautiful eyes, touching his arm with a gentle finger, stooping, even, to whisper something in his ear. His face was fixed; he seemed unmoved by her subtle tactics and yet Sara had the impression that there was something between the two . . . something intimate.

Why not? she was asking herself a short while later when she was eating freshly cooked chicken with her fingers. He was only human and, moreover, he was living primitively, so what was more natural than that he should take a mate? She glanced sideways at him, aware of the dynamic strength portrayed in his firm, clear-cut features. A virile man, undoubtedly. Her eyes strayed again to Luli, and a strange unfathomable sensation swept over her—as if she had been ruthlessly doused with icy cold water. The lovely girl was close to him again, offering him a browned, delicious slice of pig. He took it and the Native girl hovered over him as he ate it, her body beneath the sarong seductively curved, one naked breast almost touching his face.

He seemed all at once to become aware of Sara's interest and turned a wide unsmiling stare upon her. She coloured and looked away, anger rising at the arrogance of him.

'Something wrong?' Cool tones and tinged with a sort of sardonic amusement. But the hard grey eyes were still arrogant—challengingly so.

'No, of course not,' she almost snapped, aware of the keen interest on Luli's face as she listened to words she could not understand. 'What could be wrong?'

He shrugged and turned away, to say something to the chief and once again Sara was left to herself. She glanced around once more, making a mental note of all she saw, so that she could write it down later, by the light of the pressure lamp that one of the boys had hung in her tent. Several dogs were roaming about, waiting for the scraps to be thrown to them; they were kept, Muda had told her, for hunting wild boar. At the entrance to the *penghulu's* 'door' were two fine cocks, tethered by their legs. Cockfighting, she had learned, was a favourite sport of the men of the Ubani Ulu tribe. It was illegal, but they were so far from the arm of the law that they could get away with it without any trouble at all.

'More chicken——' Linjau stopped abruptly and then added, 'What is your name? I can't keep calling you "woman".'

'Miss Chesworth—Sara Chesworth.'

'Sara. . . .' He spoke the name musingly. 'Do you want some more chicken? Luli wants to know.'

'Yes, please. But I'd like a plate—or something.'

'You're not at the Hilton,' he returned with heavy sarcasm. 'You're in a longhouse, eating with the Natives, so you do as they do.'

She set her mouth at his tone, but something made her say, a curious ring to her voice,

'Do you mean to tell me that you actually enjoy picking at greasy food with your fingers?'

'I don't mean to tell you anything,' was his swift and disconcerting rejoinder. 'I thought I'd already made that clear.'

Sara drew a breath and counted ten.

'I wasn't probing, Mr—er—John. . . .'

How his name came to her lips she could never have

explained; she knew that she had thought of him as John rather than Linjau, but that was no reason for her having the audacity to address him by the name. In fact, she was as much surprised as he. She saw him scowl, saw his thin lips compress, noticed with a little apprehensive tingle that the muscles round them had flexed, that his nostrils quivered. How like a wild animal! A tiger . . . Linjau. . . .

'How the hell do you know my name?' he demanded furiously. 'I'll flog the man who's talked!'

'The *penghulu* is wondering what you're angry about,' she said in a whisper, her apprehensive gaze fixed on the lean, sun-wizened face of the chief. 'You said we hadn't to offend him, but he looks offended now.'

This seemed to calm the white man, for his features relaxed and the frown was smoothed out. Only the ice-flecked grey of his eyes remained unchanged; it sent a quivering chill down Sara's spine. To be alone with him! It would be terrifying!

'I'll talk to you later,' he said through his teeth. 'For the present, I shall have to talk to *him*.' And at that he went off into Malay and for some minutes the two men were deep in conversation. Tama and Muda came and sat beside Sara, on the other side, and chatted to her, explaining about the way of life of this particular tribe—which was, in many ways, very similar to that of other tribes of the *ulu*.

'They clear some of the jungle and grow rice,' said Muda. 'And they do all kind of things with it, including making the drink you have there——' He pointed to the cup on the floor. 'They also catch mouse-deer and trade them down river for other things like tobacco and liquor. Many of the Natives have shotguns these days——'

'Shotguns?' Sara turned to stare disbelievingly at his profile. 'Really?' She was thinking of the white man with his blowpipe and wondering why he did not own a gun.

'Yes, and they are not very wise when they use them— not always. You see, if too many pigs are killed, or wild boar or other animals, there's danger of a shortage of protein up here, and the government is trying to do something about it.'

Sara was thoughtful for a space.

'I suppose, Muda, that there's something to be said for educating these people, yet on the other hand, they're happy as they are, living the primitive life.'

Muda shrugged, his attention caught by a virile-looking youth who was fondling a young girl's shoulder. It was Tama who commented on what Sara had just said.

'I have never regretted my father's action in bringing me and my brothers and sisters away from the *ulu*, miss. I shall be a teacher one day and that is a good thing, I believe. I am very happy to look forward to getting my diploma. My father will be proud of me.'

'Yes, I expect he will.'

'I shall of course please him by wearing the ceremonial costume of my ancestors.'

'You will?' Sara blinked at him. 'But isn't that a loin-cloth——?'

'It's a cloth round here, yes, but over it there is a sort of apron at the front and the back, and round my waist I shall wear a belt.'

'And on top?'

'Only a hat, with hornbill feathers in it, and on my arms there will be bangles.'

'And you will wear that at the college, when you receive your diploma?'

'I have said so, yes.'

Muda wanted his attention and he turned, to watch the youth and the girl. The two boys said something in Malay and then laughed. This attracted the attention of both Linjau and the chief and they turned their heads. But it was at Sara that the white man's gaze was directed. His eyes narrowed slowly as he noticed her rising colour, and a sneer curled across the thin, ruthless mouth. She averted her eyes, bringing down her long lashes at the same time. An alertness gripped her, for just before her gaze left his she noticed the man's burning expression; it had entered his eyes swiftly, in a flash. Fierce and primitive, it seemed to portray a sort of wild and savage desire . . . the kind of desire that tore a man's control to shreds.

It was very late when at last the people began to move, speaking in Malay to Sara, shyly but with a broad smile on every face.

'They're saying good night and sleep well,' Linjau told her curtly. She and he had risen and were ready to leave. Tama and Muda had already gone, having asked if they might do so. The white man, overhearing the request, had said unexpectedly,

'You can let them go if you like. I'll see you back to your tent.'

Nerves alert, she had replied,

'I'd rather have the boys escort me, if you don't mind.'

'For myself, I couldn't mind a damn,' he returned unpleasantly, but went on to say that the *penghulu* had indicated that his male guest look after his female one, and he was expecting them to leave together, and even to enter his hut. 'I did warn you that he would expect us to sleep together, a procedure that's considered to end the evening happily for all——'

'I don't believe you,' she had whispered, but at that moment the chief butted in and she thought she would never know whether the translation of his words was the truth or not. 'Penghulu Mira says it will please him that we go together to my hut and you stay the night. He believes we're both willing——' He flung a hand carelessly. 'It is custom, you see, so it would be quite incomprehensible to him if we were to disappoint him. Added to that, he has in effect given us an order.' He stopped to look at her with an unfathomable expression. 'He's my chief and therefore I must make a pretence at carrying out his orders.'

Sara had said nothing, at that time believing she could manage to separate herself from the man once they were outside, in the darkness of the jungle, but now that the time to leave had arrived she seemed to have lost her nerve. There seemed to lurk so many dangers out there; she felt she would be frozen with fear if she went alone to her tent, which was some distance from the longhouse.

Goodnights were said to the chief, and to those who had not yet disappeared behind their doors.

'I'm afraid,' Linjau was saying as they reached the bottom of the ladder, 'that we shall have to go towards my hut because Penghulu Miri will be watching us from the verandah.'

'Only for a few seconds. After that he won't be able to see us.'

'I have my torch. He will naturally expect me to use it; I always do.'

She said tartly,

'You have an answer for everything, haven't you? How are we to get to my tent? I ought not to have let the boys go without me.'

She was trying to keep her voice steady, her nerves at a temperate level, so as to conceal the agitation within.

'We shall get to your tent later, when the longhouse sleeps——'

'It might be hours before everyone goes to bed!'

'We can't get to your tent by any other path than the one that runs past the longhouse,' he cut in tersely. They were on that path, but going in the opposite direction, towards his hut, which was a little way off the main path, along a narrower track overhung with the branches of ancient forest trees. 'We shall have to wait a while before venturing past again.'

'I don't want to stay in your hut!' she flashed, and almost before the last word was out he was speaking, his voice cold as tempered steel.

'That makes two of us. Do you suppose for one moment that I want a woman like you around?—a snooper obsessed with the prospect of glory?'

She subsided into an embarrassed silence. The man was hateful, she thought, and yet there still lingered at the back of her mind the conviction that he had every right to dislike her for the intruder she was, a journalist bent on getting a good story.

They walked on in silence after that, with only the beam of his torch for guidance. Sara kept close—she had to, as the path was narrow and if she were to step off it she was very likely to sink into the swampy ground, perhaps up to her knees. And she had no wish to be in the humiliating position of relying on him to get her out.

They reached the hut at last, its outline simple, blending with the primitive jungle surroundings. Linjau made no attempt to enter, but stood by the door, his eyes lifted to the dark sky above. Stars had become scarce and Sara realised that there was every likelihood of a storm.

The silence stretched, and with the passing of each moment she was becoming more and more uneasy. All she wanted was to get back to the safety of her tent, where, outside, the two Dyak boys in their own rough shelter were there to guard her. She spoke at last, the feverish alertness of her senses forcing the words from her lips.

'It isn't sensible for me to be here. I want to go back to my tent.'

'Not yet.' His body swung round so that it faced the dim outline of the longhouse. Lights could still be seen. 'In fact,' he said impatiently after a pause, 'I'm afraid we shall have to go inside. Jungle people can see in the dark, and I feel sure that Penghulu Miri is still standing where we left him.'

'But——'

'Shut up and come inside! I've told you I don't want you, so when you're thinking of the inconvenience you're being caused, think also of mine. It's a damn sight greater than yours!'

Sara swallowed, trying to get rid of the tight ball of anger that had risen in her throat.

'I'm sorry,' she managed quiveringly. 'All this is no fault of mine!'

'Then whose fault is it?' he demanded, turning as he opened the door. 'No one here asked you to come poking and prying——'

'For goodness' sake let it rest!' she just had to say. 'You've said it all before and I admit I can understand your aversion to anyone like me. But it's my job and I try to do it well.'

His hand was on the side of the door, his face in shadow.

'You can understand my aversion?' he repeated

curiously. 'You amaze me by the admission.'

'We're not all rotten!'

'Come inside,' he ordered harshly. 'Men of the jungle have exceptional hearing, too. I don't want the chief to think we're quarrelling.'

'He doesn't know why I'm here, obviously?'

'He probably does, but he knows you'll get nothing out of me. Penghulu Miri is known for his hospitality. Unless you were a criminal of some kind he wouldn't turn you away without giving a party in your honour. He has a peculiar superstition that his ancestors will be angry if he doesn't welcome strangers and offer them friendship.'

'He seems nice.' Automatically she was entering the hut, but she stood just inside the door . . . ready to turn and run if necessary.

'I'll light the lamp,' he said, ignoring her remark. 'Come in and shut the door.' He was at the other side of the hut; Sara turned to glance outside, aware of her heart pounding against her ribs. She had been in some sticky situations since working for the *Sphere*, but had never been really frightened. This man frightened her; she certainly had no wish to be alone with him in this hut, so far from her two guides.

A perfume assailed her nostrils as she stood there, irresolute, wondering if she dared make a run for it and be lucky enough to reach her tent without falling into the swamp. She sniffed appreciatively at the heady perfume of night flowers unfolded to the dark. A yellow moon sailed through clouds heavy with rain, then vanished as if suddenly dissolved into nothingness. The sky was threatening and she felt instinctively that if she did not get back to her tent soon she might not get back for some considerable time.

'I think I ought to go,' she began, and was cut short by

his exclamation of asperity.

'For God's sake, woman, do as you're told before I come over there and haul you in!'

She set her teeth, blinking as the light from the pressure lamp dispelled the blackness of the hut.

'I——'

'Do as I say!' He strode over and slammed the door closed. 'Let the chief sleep! He won't do so if he thinks there's something wrong here!'

She glared at him.

'I suppose that by "something wrong" you mean that we're not in bed together!'

Whatever had made her utter words like that! She blushed to the roots of her hair, turning from the astonished humour that pierced the grim formidability of those hard grey eyes.

'Exactly,' he murmured after a space. 'I scarcely expected to hear you say it, though. You're coming out of your shell and no mistake; it must be the influence of the jungle. Stay a bit longer and you'll be going primitive.' He paused, offering her the chance to speak, but she retained a frowning silence and glanced at the door, wishing a miracle would happen and it would open to reveal her two guides standing there, ready to take her back to the tent. 'Who told you my name?' he wanted to know presently. 'It must have been one of the Natives —At least, one of the Natives told one of your boys—for a bribe. Which one was it?'

'I have no idea,' she began, then stopped, suddenly remembering that the Native's name was Agan.

'You're a liar!' He looked at her with contempt. 'I shall find out who the man was—although I have a good idea who it was already.'

Sara gave a small sigh and said quietly,

'You spoke about punishing him. You won't—please. It wasn't his fault; the bribe as you call it must have been a great temptation to him.' She did not realise just how appealing she looked and sounded, but even if she had, it would never have occurred to her that the man's interest was caught.

'I said I'd flog him, I recall——' He looked at her from head to foot. 'I'd rather flog you for your damned impudence in coming here to spy on me! I don't see why you should escape unscathed.' No response from Sara. In fact, she was suddenly too terrified to speak, for there was that in his dark, aquiline face that was definitely evil . . . and in his intent gaze there was an expression so purposeful that she turned instinctively and opened the door. But she had no time to go through it. With a leap as swift and agile as a jungle cat he was upon her, gripping her wrist and twisting her round to face him. God, he means mischief! she thought, managing to utter a strangled cry of protest as he brought her slender body to his with a savage jerk that fetched her teeth together, trapping her tongue. His arms were about her, his lips sensuous and yet sneeringly triumphant.

Sara twisted her head this way and that, but her efforts were futile, absurdly optimistic. His strength soon reduced her puny struggles to nothing more than a cry for mercy as she begged him to let her go. His response was to grip her chin and thrust it up so that she was compelled to look at him. A terrible shudder passed through her. She felt she would rather have fallen into the hands of one of the Natives than this savage who had her in his power. His eyes glittered, as if a flame was lit within them . . . the burning flame of desire. She had seen it before, when they were in the longhouse.

'Let me go,' she pleaded, tears filling her eyes. 'I won't

b-bother ab-about the story—I—I promise——'

His lips were on hers, masterfully crushing to silence any further words she had meant to utter. She attempted again to struggle; his response this time was to grasp a handful of her hair and drag her head back with a ruthless, savage movement that brought another cry of protest and pain to her lips. His mouth crushed hers again, forcing her lips apart in a kiss so sensuous and passionate that she found herself being carried on the swell of his ardour, her own awakened desires advancing alongside his. She was lost! Dark and hopeless resignation encompassed her, and when his groping hand found her breast through the thin cotton blouse she wore her whole body thrilled to the pleasure and the pain that his brute strength inflicted.

'There's something about a white woman,' he breathed hoarsely, his lips hot and possessive against her cheek. 'I'd forgotten. . . .' Yet again his lips found hers, and the sensuous pressure of his body sent fire through her veins. She had no thoughts other than the man and his intentions; her mind was drugged by the intensity of emotions that she could neither understand nor control. She did not want to understand or to control the throbbing infection that gripped her, for its sequel was rapture untold. 'Yes, I'd forgotten . . . it's so long, and Native girls make one forget what it's like to make love to a white woman. . . .' His voice trailed to nothingness, and his arms about her tightened. He saw the dark and dreamy yearning in her eyes and gave a short, mirthless laugh. 'When it comes to the primitive desires of the flesh women are not so different. You're just as willing as any of the Native girls I've had. You'll surrender without a struggle.'

Sara froze suddenly as all the fire went out of her body.

Native girls. *Women are all the same when it comes to the needs of the flesh.* What talk was this? Yet did she suppose that an interlude of sex with her would render him loving and sentimental? It was to have been a diversion for him, an interesting experiment during which he could compare the lovemaking of a white woman with that of a Native girl.

Revolted, she wrenched herself from his arms, taking him by surprise.

'You—you—heathen!' she cried suffocatingly. 'How many Native girls have you had, that you can brag about your conquests?'

She saw the grey eyes narrow and harden, realised at once that there was no feeling within the man's mind or heart. He was a savage, a man whose instincts at this moment were entirely primitive. But his reaction to her outburst was very different from what she expected; his voice was quiet when he spoke, saying slowly,

'You resent my mention of the Native girls? Did you suppose I live the life of a saint?' Sarcasm, deep and emphasised, and tinged with sardonic amusement. Sara stood some way from him, her body still quivering from the emotional scene that had just taken place.

'The mention of the Native girls meant nothing to me,' she lied. 'Why should I, a stranger to you, resent anything you say?'

'Your surrender was close,' he said perceptively, 'but being an Englishwoman, with totally impractical ideas regarding sex, you hated the thought that I'd had Native girls——'

'My—surrender was *not* close!' she denied hotly. 'What an opinion you have of yourself! If anything—anything had happened. . . .' She trailed off, embarrassment sweeping over her, and she looked away, avoiding his gaze.

He laughed softly and moved closer to her.

'By "anything" I presume you meant a little love scene?'

Her embarrassment grew, but she did turn her eyes towards him as she replied,

'It would have been without my—er—co-operation.'

A low laugh escaped him.

'You mean—without your reciprocation?' The straight dark brows lifted fractionally. 'Liar!' He stood over her now, cool and confident . . . and indescribably dangerous. 'If you were honest you'd admit that even at this moment your thoughts, your body, perceive their master.'

'Oh——! You're hateful!' Her eyes flashed scorn at him, but she was fighting mentally to deny the truth o what he had said. She would have liked to deny too that his magnetism drew her in a way she would never have believed possible, that his attraction for her was there from the start. 'Let me out of here!' she cried, stepping back towards the door. 'You'll be in trouble with the Sarawak authorities if you molest me!'

Again that low laugh as his hand came out to grip her wrist.

'There'll be no question of my molesting you,' he told her confidently. 'You'll participate willingly.' His hand tightened upon her wrist; she was drawn to his body, and eyes that were half mocking sought her face, mastery and arrogance within their depths. His arms became hawsers of steel as she began to struggle and she gave up, to lean limply against him, the blood drumming in her ears. She felt her heart throb with expectation as he bent his head, waited in a torment of anticipation for his kiss, for the arrogant, masterful caress of his hands. As before her mind was drugged; she had lost touch with everything save the man whose dominance and strength were reducing her to willing submission. She knew he must be gloating, that tomorrow his sneers would reveal exactly what he thought of her, yet in spite of all this she was unable to fight, and when his lips came down on hers in a kiss of brutal disrespect, she found herself responding, and straining her body to his even without invitation.

He paused a moment and she raised her eyes quickly, to see smouldering embers of passion in his. The next moment she was swept up into his arms and carried to the low couch that was his bed. It was narrow; he laughed and said as he laid her down,

'There isn't much room . . . but we shan't need much, shall we?'

He went over to the lamp and Sara waited for the darkness that would come with his extinguishing the light. And then there was a flash, followed instantly by a crack of thunder that split the silence. The man turned, his face expressionless.

'We're in for a storm,' he said, 'a bad one.' He seemed restless, undecided; his eyes rested on the lamp for a moment before he turned away.

'Oh. . . .' Sara could think of nothing else to say. She felt as if she were suddenly alone here, for he was far away, unreachable. The change in him was dramatic; he had a cold unemotional air about him and the recent occurrences might never have taken place. 'There hasn't been a night storm since I came,' she said at last, actually jumping when another crack of thunder ripped through the silence.

'We have thunderstorms of great intensity in this part of the world, and many of them occur during the early hours after midnight.'

'It—will last a long time?' She was sitting on the edge

of the couch, her eyes on the man's tall lean frame. He looked at her with an expression of indifference that hurt. Why should she be hurt? The answer was avoided for the present, but she strongly suspected that it would have to be answered some time.

'All through the night, probably—and fifteen or twenty inches of rain could fall.'

He stood very still, thoughtful, remote . . . and looking at her with an odd expression in his eyes.

Thunder cracked again, following instantly on the lightning. And then the first spots of rain fell on to the roof of the hut.

'It'll be a deluge within minutes.' His voice was sharp now, and he was no longer remote. 'You'll have to sleep in the longhouse. Come on, we'll have to hurry!'

She moved at the command, assuring herself that she welcomed the escape. But within seconds her mood changed and she was affected again by his physical magnetism, by his undoubted power over her which she had to admit was the call of the master. She knew again the wild craving for the touch of his lean brown fingers, the savage contact of his lips with hers. She wanted nothing more than to be alone with him . . . dangerously aware of him as a man. She found herself saying in a low and diffident little voice,

'Why the longhouse? I mean. . . .' Her voice trailed as a modicum of pride forced itself into her consciousness.

The sudden smile on his face was light to her in the midst of this rising storm.

'You'd rather be here, in the hut?' She did not answer and he continued, his tone oddly gentle, 'I've said that the storm could last throughout the night and that an enormous amount of rain could fall, and probably will.

You wouldn't get back if we left it—at least, you'd not get back in the morning early, owing to the floods that are bound to occur. The river'll be a torrent with its waters flowing on to the banks. No, you must go to the longhouse. I'll take you at once.'

'Why not my tent?'

'A tent's no place to be in the kind of storm that we're going to have.'

She was standing close, and she lifted her eyes to his; he frowned suddenly and drew an impatient breath—as if he were troubled in some way by his own particular thoughts.

She was tempting him and he knew it. Savagely he caught her to him and for one moment she knew the ecstasy of his embrace, his kiss, before, almost flinging her from him, he strode to the door and flung it wide.

'Be quick,' he ordered brusquely. 'It's raining hard already!'

CHAPTER FIVE

SARA awoke to a feeling of deep dejection. She had slept in the longhouse, on a rush mat and covered with one of the bright hand-woven blankets which the Native women made so beautifully and which were an important item of exchange with the traders downstream. Linjau—who had surprised her by saying she could call him John—had obviously found some feasible explanation for the request that she should sleep in the longhouse. She could not understand what he was saying to the chief, of course, but she judged by the *penghulu*'s expression, and his gestures, that the storm was being discussed. His face was a study as he looked from one to the other, and he seemed to put a few questions to John. Sara, filled with embarrassment, convinced herself that the chief was wanting to know if they had 'lain together' and if so, what did the man think of the woman. However, as nothing was to be read from John's face or understood from his words, Sara decided to put her uneasiness and embarrassment at one side, resolving to get a good night's sleep. This she did, rather to her surprise, but on wakening she felt this flood of depression, brought on by the instant recollection of what had taken place the night before in the white man's hut. What must he think of her? It ought not by rights to matter, she told herself . . . but it did matter. She would like to have his respect, his admiration . . . and his love . . .?

She sat up, with the sensation that all the blood in her body was rushing to her heart. She wanted desperately to deny it, but the bald fact persisted. She had fallen wildly, crazily in love with a man whom she ought to have despised, because he was a shirker, a man who had not had the courage to face up to whatever the disaster was that had overtaken him. It was herself she despised, hating the emotions that had taken hold of her. She, a sensible, level-headed woman with years of experience on a newspaper behind her, to fall like a green girl just out of the schoolroom, a teenager eager for her first romance.

'I shall fight it!' she told herself vehemently, and the next moment was adding, 'I shall have to, since he would never want me anyway.'

With the resolve gaining strength as the morning hours passed, she made another resolve, which was to get her story, and her pictures. John did not deserve consideration after all, simply because of his intention to take her, to grasp the diversion her weakness offered. He was ruthless and she could be the same, and if it meant antagonism and combat—well, she was confident that she could take care of herself ... so long as she avoided a situation like that of last night.

She got up, and was given rice biscuits for breakfast. She would rather have gone to her tent and let the boys prepare her some coffee and toast, but she prudently accepted what the women of the longhouse offered, conscious of the fact that she must never refuse anything that was given her to eat or drink.

She saw the *penghulu* before she left the longhouse and thanked him graciously for his hospitality. It was while she was doing this that John put in an appearance, staying only long enough to say a few words to the chief. He spoke in Malay; Sara, watching the Native's expression, knew even before he spoke that she was being sent away from the village. John looked at her after the chief had finished and said,

'Penghulu Miri says you must leave this village immediately.'

She drew a breath.

'This is your doing,' she accused, and he nodded at once, the grey eyes narrowed and sneeringly triumphant.

'I have no need to tell you why I want you away from here,' he said. 'You're a nuisance to me and I want you out of it.'

No reference to last night—not even by a look. It meant nothing to him—but then why should it? She had coloured vividly at the sight of him, but he had ignored her embarrassment and she doubted if he had even noticed it.

She left the longhouse and made her way through the water and mud to the boat. Tama and Muda were busy underneath it, freeing the bottom from the tangle of weeds that had swirled around it during the storm. Sara wanted her camera, wondering if it would be completely ruined by the torrential and prolonged rainfall that had occurred throughout the early hours of the morning. She was flat, depressed, and uncertain of her next move. On the surface her only course seemed to be that of returning home and admitting failure. But that went so much against the grain that her mind immediately began to work in other directions. She could stay, of course, living on the boat, but that would not do her much good at all. The other alternative was to go to other villages and glean what she could about the white man, but again that course seemed to present little prospect of success, since the word would soon get around all the villages that the Natives must not talk about the white man.

'What are we doing today?' Tama wanted to know when he and Muda had finished clearing the boat to their satisfaction.

'I don't know, Tama. I haven't had much success up till now.' She thought again of the camera and the one solitary photograph she had taken of John. It was probably ruined, anyway, unless by some miracle the undergrowth where the camera was hidden was so well protected by the trees that no real soaking had occurred. How to get back, though, with all this mud about, and in addition the order of the village chief that she must leave right away. She finally reached the conclusion that she would have to wait until dark before she dared venture past the longhouse again.

The day passed so slowly that she could have screamed. Never had a consignment proved so unprofitable as this. With grim determination she had always managed to get her story, but determination was worthless in a situation like this. Perhaps she should have worked secretly, not saying that she was a journalist, for it did seem, right from the first, that the man in question would never talk. But she had been optimistic about gaining information from the Natives, and in addition being able to take photographs without the man knowing.

At last darkness began to fall; the jungle creatures that fed by night began to make themselves heard—the owls and the tree frogs, the civet cat and the hill otters. In the pure purple sky stars gradually appeared, but it was not fully dark when Sara left the *prahu*. She felt a little apprehensive about going out in the pitch dark, and felt that if she went with stealth she would find it possible to mingle with the shadows and make her way successfully to the place where her camera was hidden.

Tama and Muda were to follow but to stay some distance behind, and not to reveal themselves unless something happened that made it necessary.

She had managed to get safely past the longhouse when to her consternation and annoyance she saw John standing in the middle of a little clearing, a tall gaunt figure in the swiftly-gathering darkness, an immobile figure that seemed to be part of the jungle landscape rather than a human being. She stopped, glanced around, but saw nothing of her two guides. She was in the shadows of jungle trees; they hid, in their foliage, the hated leeches, and cockchafers, to say nothing of the rhinoceros and stag beetles that abound in the jungle places. A slight shiver passed along her spine, for the whole aspect was eerie, primitive as the dawn of time.

Suddenly the gaunt figure seemed to stiffen. No sound came to her ears as the man moved. He swung around and she could almost imagine every sense being on the alert, could almost read the question in his brain. Something alien was about. Sara wondered if he had become so animal-like that his nose could pick up the scent of anything that was in the vicinity. She dared not move even a muscle, but just stood there in the shadows, the feverish alertness of her own senses setting her heart pounding against her ribs.

He moved again, to tread the ground noiselessly with his bare feet. He was in a loincloth, she now made out, and even in the dimness his body gleamed like an image carved out of polished wood. He suddenly leapt forward at the same time flashing a torch he had been carrying but which she never saw.

'You!' he exclaimed seconds later as he gripped the front of her blouse and brought her unceremoniously from her hiding-place. 'What the hell are you up to now!'

She could scarcely speak for the fear that blocked her throat, but she did manage to stammer out a few words as she said,

'I—I was j-just taking a—a stroll——'

'Don't lie! You were intending to snoop again!' He gave her a savage thrust, then brought her back, still gripping her blouse. Furious now, she twisted her body, knocking his hand, and managed to free herself

'You're so clever, aren't you? I was not intending any such thing!' Her eyes flashed as he shone his torch into them. 'I can take a walk if I like, surely, without your coming to the conclusion that I'm intending to peep through the chinks in that tumbledown hut you live in!' She stopped and frowned inwardly at what she had said. If he chose to live in a hut what right had she to say disparaging things about it? He was glowering at her, her words adding tinder to his wrath.

'It would be more than your life's worth if I caught you peeping through chinks!' he assured her smoulderingly. 'You do realise that if I handed you over to Penghulu Miri you'd be kept prisoner until such time as he decided to let you free?'

She swallowed.

'You wouldn't——'

'Scared you, have I?' He gave a short, mirthless laugh. 'It would do you good to find yourself a prisoner. . . .' He shone the torch over her, examining her body calculatingly, and her breath seemed to stop in her throat. If he should tempt her. . . . Fury rose again, fury at the knowledge of her own weakness. To have fallen in love with such a creature, a heathen who went about almost naked, who had no further time or wish for the ordinary refinements which had come with civilisation!

'I'll go . . .' she began, moving away. But he shot out a hand to grip her wrist.

'Oh no, you don't. It's early yet and you've time to come back again and do the snooping you intended. I'm just debating on whether to make you the *penghulu*'s prisoner, or mine.' A small pause as he shone the torch again to make another unveiled examination of her body. Then his eyes moved to her throat . . . and her head. She shivered even before he spoke.

'I rather think I'd like to see that head of yours dangling on the end of a piece of string—or perhaps they'd put it in a hanging-basket along with those other human skulls you saw——' He stopped, his lips quirking. 'Makes you shiver, eh? Well, don't panic at this stage. I shan't hand you over yet. We'll go into the hut you despised and resume what was interrupted last night.'

'No!' Sara twisted, but this time there was no escape for her. In the light from the torch's beam as he swung it

to one side, she saw that his lips were drawn back from
his teeth, that his grey eyes burned with fire, like a
tiger's in the dark. 'Oh, let me go!'

But he had her up in his hold, swinging her from the
ground in one simple and easy movement, and she was
borne along in his arms, his feet in the silent jungle
making not the slightest sound.

She shouted for the two boys, but they did not come
and she knew that they would not obey any summons she
might make. They were there, within earshot; they had
seen what was happening but, as before, they were
afraid of interfering. It was useless to have them as
protectors, she thought, but swift upon this she was
admitting, as she had admitted before, that they were
merely safeguarding their jobs. In any case, they had
learned, since coming up here and talking to many
Natives, that the Englishman was esteemed by all the
tribes and their leaders and therefore there might be
trouble for anyone who molested him in any way.
Another thing—Tama and Muda had been provided
only as guides; it had not been supposed that they would
be needed as protectors—unless it was against animals or
other hazards of the jungle.

He entered the hut, kicking the door shut behind him,
then set Sara on her feet. She wheeled swiftly, hoping to
get to the door and escape, taking him by surprise. But
she might have known that a man like him, with the
instincts he had acquired over the years, would never be
taken by surprise. He gripped her arm without any
attempt at gentleness and swung her round against him.
And before she knew it his lips were crushing hers,
brutally and without the smallest degree of respect.

'There's something about a white woman that the
Native woman hasn't got.' Moving away abruptly, he

motioned her to sit down on the truckle bed, but she backed away, watching him light the pressure lamp.

Amusement shot into his expression as he turned.

'All right, then, on the chair——' He flicked a hand, but she shook her head.

'Kindly let me out of here,' she said. 'I'll promise to go back to the boat and stay there.'

'Why didn't you obey the chief's orders?' he asked, ignoring her request and the promise that went with it.

'That's my business.'

His grey eyes narrowed.

'You had the *prahu* hidden somewhere, obviously.'

'Are you going to let me out of here?'

'Yes . . . when I've finished with you. Sit down!'

She looked at him, wishing with all her heart she had not bothered about the camera—which would, in all probability, not be worth rescuing anyway.

'If you——'

'I said, sit down.' Soft the order, but she had to obey it, sinking nervelessly on to the chair, which was more like a stool with arms, and it was made from bamboo.

'You're safe for a while,' he assured her with dry humour. 'I've been stung with something and must give myself a little first-aid.'

'Stung?' she repeated. 'What with?'

'If I knew I'd have said so. There are a hundred and one things one can be stung with in a jungle.'

'Then why stay? I'm sure you've no need to.'

He was at a sort of cupboard which was fastened to the wall, but at her words he turned around.

'Still trying?' he commented with brittle mockery. 'I've told you, Sara, to save your breath.'

His voice was quiet now, untinged with anger. He seemed to be absorbed in some thoughts of his own and turned from her once more, to open the cupboard door and take out an earthenware jar.

She stared at him, vitally aware of his attractions—of the deceptive leanness of his gaunt frame, of his long limbs covered with strong dark hair, of his gleaming shoulders and back, of the loincloth he was wearing, his only garment. A savage. . . . A man who had voluntarily thrown off the cloak of civilisation in favour of the free life, the trammelled existence he had once lived. But why? There was a reason, and how she longed to know what it was! And not merely as a piece of headline-catching news. No, she wanted to know all about him for other reasons; he intrigued her because he attracted her. Would he ever return to the old life? It seemed impossible to form a picture of him remaining here, living to be a wizened old sun-bitten man like Penghulu Miri and others she had seen since coming up into the seething, humid jungle of Borneo.

No, more easily could she picture him as the cultured country squire, or a distinguished businessman. She looked at the hand holding the jar, at the other which was closed round the lid. Brown hands, with long sensitive fingers.

She said at last, her eyes still on him as he extracted some kind of ointment from the jar after undoing the lid,

'What do you do at night? It must be terribly boring for you—in this place all the time.'

His lips curled, but he did not look at her.

'I suppose,' he said thoughtfully, 'that even a small amount of information would be welcome now. You'd have something to add to and embellish until it bears not the remotest resemblance to the truth.' He smeared the ointment on to a place above his wrist and added when she made no comment, 'The trash that you people write is incredible. Sensationalism is what you thrive on, living by your wits at the expense of your fellow-men.'

Something in the way he uttered those words, in the way they were spat out in a voice vibrating with hate, jerked Sara to alert interest.

'You've—er—suffered at the hands of the Press?'

He made no immediate answer, appearing to be fully absorbed by his task as, having rubbed in the ointment, he reached for a small box from which he took a dressing.

'How long have you been a journalist?' he wanted to know presently, as, having fixed the adhesive dressing, he replaced the box and closed the cupboard door.

'Seven years.'

Turning, he looked her over, from her shining hair to her beautiful face, and she knew he was making a mental guess at her age. She watched the gradual change in his expression, knew for sure that his thoughts had turned to desire, and a little access of fear swelled within her. Never had she met such a dangerous man! Why hadn't she tried more carefully to visualise what this trip would entail, what the hazards and the dangers were likely to be? Looking back now she was staggered by the way she had so eagerly accepted the job, blithely expecting to sail through unscathed, as she had always done before. She watched him still, thinking of the miracle that had saved her last night, but half admitting to a sense of disappointment at her salvation. Tonight, though, she was fully sane, alive to the dangers of allowing herself to be affected by his savage and primitive lovemaking.

'You're a beautiful woman,' he observed at last. 'Why aren't you married?'

She coloured at his flattery even though it was delivered with a sort of mocking satire that revealed his opinion of her, of what lay beneath the beauty.

'I haven't met the right man,' she replied, avoiding his gaze. He moved with that lightning step he had and tilted her chin, roughly, imperiously.

'Why did you look away?' he demanded, his eyes boring into hers in the most searching scrutiny she had ever known.

'I didn't——'

'Liar! Last night you found me attractive,' he said, little or no expression in his tone. 'Why haven't you met the right man? Is it that you're the kind of woman who wants someone . . . different?'

'Don't be absurd!' she flashed. 'You——'

'Obviously you caught on to my meaning,' he broke in with a trace of amusement. 'Some women are hard to please; they crave the savage kind of lover.' Releasing her chin, he walked to the other side of the hut, from where he stood, looking at her. She was hotter than before, affected profoundly by his words, because—though she hated to admit it—they were true.

But they were only true because she had met *him*, the finest specimen of manhood she had ever seen, a man of strength and power, a man whose magnetism had affected her the moment she set eyes on him. And now that magnetism was drawing her and she was fighting against it; she looked at his sensuous mouth and immediately felt those kisses, kisses that had thrilled her through and through for all their brutality. She looked at his hands and felt them on her again, arrogantly caressing . . . and his body . . . A frame of incredible strength, hard and sinewed, it had pressed to hers with that sort of exquisite pain that robs a woman of her resistance . . . and makes her crave for more.

The silence stretched intolerably and Sara had to break it, asking again to be allowed to leave. She was on a knife-edge, vague about his intentions because although at first he seemed intent on doing her a mischief, he was now adopting an attitude of near indifference.

'Do you really want to go?' There was a sort of dry humour in the smile he produced, and it was reflected in the glance he sent at her. 'Last night you'd have stayed—willingly—— No, don't deny it!' he said imperiously. 'I'm not a fool.'

Sara's eyes blazed.

'What an opinion you have of yourself!' Her eyes swept his near-naked body. 'Do you really believe you have sex appeal, looking like that?'

She held her breath, staggered by her temerity in voicing words like those. To her surprise he merely laughed and said,

'I don't know about that, Sara; what I do know is that *you* have more than enough sex appeal for any man.' His eyes were laughing and in spite of her discomfiture she could appreciate his attractiveness. What would he be like dressed in a white linen suit, or evening dress with a snow-white shirt, or even casual slacks and one of those draped-line jackets which clothes-conscious men were wearing these days?

She ventured a question even though she fully expected a snub rather than an answer.

'How long is it since you decided to give up the civilised life?' She remembered that Agan had told Tama that he thought it was about six or seven years since the white man had come to Borneo, but then Tama had gone on to say that time was not troubled about in this part of the world.

'Long enough for me to have lost the desire to return,' he answered brusquely.

'So—you will stay here for ever?' Her spirits sank and

even though she knew it was ridiculous that she should feel like this she was powerless to do anything about it.

'Perhaps not with this particular tribe, but certainly I shall stay in this part of the world.'

She was surprised that he would talk to her, and still more surprised at his attitude, which had changed rather dramatically in the last few moments. The fire had gone from his eyes and, incredible as it seemed, Sara was now convinced that he meant her no harm. What had made him change his mind? Even as the question was asked she saw him flinch; her eyes fell to the dressing and she realised he was in pain.

So that was it! She was saved again. Well, there was little probability of his objecting to her departure, she decided, getting up from the chair and saying,

'I'm going. . . .' She turned her head as the door swung inwards on its well-worn leather hinges, her eyes opening wide. Standing there was a slender Native girl with dark dreamy eyes and a sort of magical, bewitching beauty in her scantily-clothed body. She stopped on seeing Sara and her eyes went questioningly to John.

She spoke in Malay and he answered, softly, gently and with a smile. Sara, fascinated by the way he looked at the girl, could only stare, a little dazed by her beauty, but at the same time embarrassed by the fact that she was clothed only from the waist down, the bright sarong reaching almost to her bare feet.

John glanced at Sara, as if making a comparison. She had to speak, to ask who the girl was. A small silence followed before he answered quietly,

'My wife.'

'Your . . . wife?' repeated Sara hollowly, the vision of Luli flashing before her eyes, and recalling that she had been convinced that there was something between her and John. He was nodding his head slowly.

'Yes, my wife. Her name's Sri——' He beckoned her, indicating that she must stay, for she had half turned, as if she meant to leave, seeing that he was not alone. He spoke in the language she could understand and a lovely smile broke. He slid an arm about her when she approached him, his fingers resting just below her naked breast. Sara moved towards the door. John did not speak and as she reached it she turned, unable to suppress what was in her mind.

'When you first brought me here it was your intention to try—to—to make love to me. Would you have done that, knowing your wife might come in?'

His eyes lit with sardonic amusement.

'I'd have made sure the door was fixed,' he assured her, and as she stepped through the door, 'I rather think I shall be safe from your snooping for the rest of tonight.'

Closing the door, Sara stood for a moment, her cheeks burning as his words rang in her ears.

Hateful creature! Had it really been his intention to make love to her, knowing his Native wife was likely to come? Sara's mind went to the sting he had received, and her conviction that it was giving him some pain. Well, whether it was giving him pain or not, he seemed happy to have his wife with him for the night.

All thoughts of rescuing her camera were forgotten as, with a sense of brooding oppression, she slowly made her way back along the swampy path to the little river cove where the *prahu* was moored. The night was very dark, with fireflies glowing, and moon moths flitting about, touching her face and hair. Something much larger moved in a branch above her head—a tarsier, she guessed, looking for chijaks—the geckos which were its favourite food. She had never seen one of these delightful creatures, which resembled the bush-baby of Africa, but Muda had told her they were often kept as pets by people living in Kuching and other towns. The harsh cry of a nightjar pierced the silence, adding its own particular atmosphere to the awe-inspiring mystery of this Equatorial jungle. She reached the *prahu* at last, then swung around, every nerve alert.

'You. . . .' Her quivering body settled at once as she saw the two Dyak boys appear like wraiths from the undergrowth bordering the mango swamp by the river's edge.

'We followed as you said,' began Tama, an excuse on his lips. Sara, tired and dispirited, her mind in a whirl-pool of emotions, with the vision of Sri and John alone in the hut spinning before her eyes, told the boys that it did not matter that they had failed to come to her rescue. They seemed relieved and, after seeing her on to the boat where she intended spending the night, they left her and, with the noiseless movements of the jungle-born, dis-appeared into the night. They were not far away, though, their rough shelter having been constructed on a rocky limestone ledge close to the bank of the stream.

CHAPTER SIX

THERE was nothing for it, decided Sara the following morning, but to abandon the project and return to England. It would be her first failure, but she supposed there had to be one some time. Joe would be disappointed, but he would get over it. Sara thought of his infatuation for her and hoped he had got over that already.

The sun had come up early, its first low rays colouring the jungle jade-green and bringing the mountains into sharp silhouette against the oyster sky. Noise and hidden movement filled the atmosphere as the vast and varied jungle population began to stir, after that eerie interlude of silence when the night-feeding creatures had gone to rest. Sara was fascinated by the whole mysterious aspect of the jungle, and the idea of leaving it so soon was almost as depressing as the picture which she was having so much difficulty in blotting out—that of John and his lovely Native wife, Sri.

But she did put it out of her mind as, washing in the water provided by Tama, she dressed in denims and a long-sleeved shirt. For it was a profitless way to occupy her thought process, and she concentrated on what was going on around her as the sun rose higher in the sky. Everywhere there was vigorous life, and between dawn and dusk every day the jungle at all levels was alive with the noise of thousands of insects. She had been told by the Dyak boys that Borneo had more than five hundred kinds of birds and two hundred species of animals. She wished she had time to stay and see more of these creatures. Up till now she had glimpsed the orang-utan, the ape that was closest to man and was sadly becoming so rare that it was only by the greatest good luck that she had seen one. In the mangrove swamp she had one day seen a proboscis monkey, and she had seen several other species of monkey including the gibbon.

Of the flowers that abounded she loved the orchids, for most of the other flowers lacked colour. Beneath the great trees of the primary forest there were to be seen a few delicately-coloured foliage plants, terrestrial and epiphytic ferns of all shapes and sizes, mosses, ginger plants and some others. Along the river banks were clearings now and then, where flourished many flowering shrubs, but their colours were dominated by pinks and yellows with little variety of other hues. There were many picture plants, whose method of nutrition was by snaring ants and other insects, drowning and digesting them in the liquid contained in the body of the plant. This particular plant did have beautiful colours, a most vital necessity in attracting the insects.

The sound of cocks crowing in the muddy ground beneath the slatted floor of the longhouse brought home to Sara that the Natives would be moving already, and she gave a sigh of impatience with herself for not stirring before now, as she must go and find her camera. She spoke to Tama, telling him of her intention. Both he and Muda had been far from happy at remaining here after the order given by the *penghulu*, but Sara had known that he would neither take her prisoner nor have her murdered. Head-hunting had ceased a long time ago and it was known that the Natives were most friendly towards travellers, welcoming them to their villages and giving a feast in their honour. Sara *had* met with unfriendliness, though, but knew it was owing to the Natives' loyalty to the white man who had elected to make his home in their midst.

'I must get my camera,' she told Tama when he seemed to frown when she told him that they would not be leaving just yet. 'Follow me, at a distance.' She grimaced to herself as she gave this order, since neither boy was any good to her in an emergency. However, it was wise to have them close if only to translate for her if she should encounter the tribal chief.

She decided to have her breakfast first, seeing that

Muda had made the coffee and Tama had produced a couple of fried sausages, some packet toast, and butter from a tin.

She heard the glorious song of the yellow-crowned bulbul as she came from the boat to make her way along the path which would lead her to the place where her camera was hidden, and wondered how a diet of snails could produce such trilling runs of music. The magpie-robin's call was far less spectacular, as was that of the vivid-coloured barbets, their blues and greens and crimsons flashing in the sunlight. From the mountain-side—and indeed from all parts of the surrounding jungle—came a succession of wild birds; parrots and broadbills, egrets and woodpeckers, and the exquisite sunbirds and flower-peckers.

From the longhouse all kinds of noises could be heard, and as she neared it the smell of cooking drifted to her, but already some of the men were working on some cleared ground, tending the *padi* they had sown.

She had managed to pass the longhouse without being observed, having kept to the dense cover of the jungle vegetation and drapery, when suddenly she heard the sharp and urgent cry of warning from one of her boys.

'What——?' Terror caught her throat and her voice collapsed as, her eyes dilating, she saw the vicious creature making directly for her, having emerged from a steaming mass of vegetation to the left of where she was walking. A strangled scream escaped her; she put up her hands to protect her face, vaguely aware of shouts of concern, of brown women and children running about or calling from the verandah of the longhouse. She tried to move, but terror held her rooted to the spot. The honey bear, Sarawak's only dangerous animal, had been known to be a killer, especially if it happened to have young. This one, a large and magnificent creature, reared on its hind legs and another scream rent the air as its merciless claws ripped at her flesh. Again and again she screamed, then began to moan softly, sure that she was about to die, for no one seemed to have the courage to come to her rescue. She was writhing about in agony, crouched face downwards on the muddy ground, when all at once the clawing ceased. With consciousness drifting from her she was lifted into someone's arms, and carried through a small crowd of gaping Natives. . . .

She regained consciousness to the immediate knowledge that she had been saved from death by a miracle. As her eyes began to focus she realised she was in John's hut, and no sooner had she moved her head than a familiar voice asked,

'How are you feeling?'

'I'm—alive-——' She winced with pain, putting a hand to her chest. A further exploration revealed that she had been stripped and that dressings had been applied to her wounds. She did not know how expertly this had been done until later. 'I'm alive,' she said again. 'And I have you to thank.' Instinctively she knew it was he who had saved her . . . and he who had stripped her and bandaged the wounds.

His tawny face was above her, an enigmatical expression in his hard grey eyes. He was wearing khaki shorts and a navy blue shirt with the sleeves rolled up above the elbows. There was a smell of disinfectant in the hut, but it mingled with the subtle aroma of pineapples drifting in through the open door, and the more earthy smell of the forest after rain.

'I expect you're ready for a drink,' said John.

'Yes, please.'

He went away, but was back directly carrying a beaker of water.

'I know you're parched,' he said, 'but drink it slowly.' He sounded stern, with a quality about him that savoured of the professional, a man by no means unused to what he was now doing. He eased her to a sitting position, noticing the dark shadows beneath her eyes.

'Have I been badly mauled?' she asked, unable to assess the extent of her injuries because, although she had believed that every part of her body except her face and head had been affected, she was experiencing very little pain.

John surprised her by saying,

'It's not nearly so bad as it seems to you at this moment. It could have been a great deal worse.' His voice was crisp, with anger in its depths. 'Why weren't your boys armed with shotguns?'

'I don't know—well,' she amended, 'I wouldn't expect them to be. They're only guides.'

'They should have been prepared for a contingency such as this.'

She let that pass, saying that if he had not appeared she would have been killed.

'How did you get it away from me——?' She broke off, shuddering at the memory.

'I killed it with a parang. Several others had fetched their parangs by that time, so you'd have been saved anyway.' He watched her drinking the water. 'Go slowly,' he ordered. 'Your thirst will be quenched just the same.'

She had been drinking thirstily, but she did as she was told and began to sip the water. She was very close to tears, but managed to hold them back. But a terrible shuddering assailed her, affecting every single part of her body. Reaction, she thought, shock. She tried to imagine him tackling that ferocious beast with the parang, the machete-like knife, or sword, used by the Natives for just about everything that required chopping, such as cutting paths through the jungle, chopping wood for the fires, and, in the past, for fighting their enemies, and for severing heads from bodies. She could imagine John wielding one with the same finesse as any of those born to it, could in fact imagine his making a success of anything he cared to tackle.

But at one time in his life he had failed at something. For surely only a failure could have driven him here, to take up a life so different from that to which he had been used. She wondered how old he was, but found it impossible to hazard a guess. He was over thirty and under forty, she estimated, but a more accurate guess was not easy.

He took the beaker from her; she suddenly thought of Sri and to her amazement she started to cry. Shock, she thought again, trying vainly to stem the tears.

'There's nothing to cry about,' he said. 'You'll recover in due course.'

'Can I be taken to the hospital at Kuching?'

He shook his head at once.

'You're not fit to be moved.'

She bit her lip, distressed.

'I don't want to be a bother to you,' she quivered, taking a corner of the blanket to dry her eyes.

'It's a bit late now for remorse,' he returned admonishingly. 'If you'd obeyed the orders of the *penghulu* it would never have happened.'

'I've already thought of that,' she admitted bleakly. And then, after a pause in which she examined the stern set features and the hardness of his eyes, 'You're angry, aren't you?' she queried in a small voice. She was certainly not herself, feeling small and weak and helpless like this. She supposed that being an unwelcome guest in this man's home was adding enormously to her depression.

'I can scarcely be expected to be pleased,' he returned with some asperity.

He was heartless! And for a moment she wondered why he had not let the animal finish her off. She would have been out of his way then, and that was what he wanted. He asked her if she had not been warned about the honey bear before she came up into the *ulu*.

'I'd heard of them,' she admitted, but went on to say that she never expected they would come out into the open as that one had done.

'They don't, usually, but that one had young. They're exceedingly vicious when they're feeding young.' He paused a moment. 'They had to be killed, as otherwise they would have died slowly, of hunger.'

'I suppose they looked adorable,' she said, but, feeling the way she was feeling at present, she had no pity in her heart for the baby bears which, she knew, were great favourites at any zoo.

'They certainly looked pretty . . . and it was hard to kill them.'

She flashed him a glance of surprise.

'That sounds strange, coming from you,' she murmured.

'You believe I've no heart, is that it?'

She let that pass. In any case, he was touching her forehead and she saw with a little feeling of uneasiness that a heavy frown had settled on his dark forbidding brow.

What was wrong? She knew her forehead was damp, but that hardly seemed to be serious enough to bring a frown like that to his face.

She heard him sigh, then he was saying with a touch of impatience,

'I hope you're not going to have a fever.'

A fever. . . .

'How long shall I be here?' she wanted to know, thrusting out such a calamity as a fever.

'That all depends,' was his unsatisfactory answer. 'I've sent your two guides back to Kuching, as they weren't doing any good up here. Penghulu Miri didn't want them; he considered they'd be a danger to our girls.'

Our girls. . . . So it would appear that he considered himself to be a full member of the Ubani Ulu tribe.

'It seems,' she said bleakly, 'that I'm to be here for some time.'

'It's your own fault,' he told her callously. 'Career women are all the same—defiant, obstinate, refusing to take advice from anyone, much less an order. You may not know it, but the *penghulu*'s furious at your disobedience. He says you've upset the omen birds.'

'Omen birds?'

'They're called "*isits*", and they're regarded as messengers of the gods. Today one of these birds flew across the river from left to right, which is an unfavourable omen according to the Ubani Ulu tribe. Also, a *kedaman*—which looks rather like a scarecrow but is for attracting birds, not scaring them away—fell down this morning: another unfavourable omen.'

Sara had gone paler even than she was before.

'What will happen?'

'I haven't heard yet. Penghulu Miri will probably consult the *bomah* and see what he has to say.'

'The *bomah*?' she repeated, sending him an interrogating glance.

'The witch-doctor.'

'Oh. . . .' A pause ensued while she thought of this, and began to recall some of the incidents related to her by the two Dyak boys as they travelled up the river in the *prahu*. 'It's all superstition,' she said defensively at length. 'I expect hundreds of birds fly over the river from left to right—and up and down, for that matter.'

His eyes narrowed.

'It might be superstition to you,' he snapped, 'but to these people it's a serious business! They're expecting bad luck—and the fault will be put down to you!'

A tug of fear caught her nerves.

'What will they—they do to me?'

'Nothing while you're under my protection.'

Relief brought a long, outdrawn breath from her lips.

'You'll keep me here until I can be taken down to Kuching?'

'As there doesn't seem to be any alternative—yes!'

'I'm sorry—for everything,' she said contritely.

'You're more sorry that you didn't get a story, though.'

Without thinking she said,

'I shall have a story—not the big one I came for, but certainly a story.'

Again the grey eyes narrowed, and the sensuous mouth was harsh suddenly.

'I could kill you and no one would know. You must be aware of that?'

There was evil in his face and she shuddered.

'You saved my life,' she reminded him, 'so you'd hardly want to kill me now.'

'Don't come to any wrong conclusions. Here in this primitive part of the jungle you're among savages—oh, yes, the Ubani Ulu are still savages in spite of their apparent friendliness and in spite of the fact that so many of the tribes have of recent years become civilised. We up here are a law unto ourselves. We might come under the jurisdiction of the Sarawak Government, but we're too far away from Kuching, too remote in our jungle fastness to be affected by its laws. Life here among the pagans is not valued very much at all, and if I feel you're going to embarrass me in any way whatsoever, I shall not hesitate to kill you.'

So calm the tone! Did he really mean it? Sara was sceptical all at once . . . and yet. . . . She looked at him searchingly; his face was a mask, unmoving even to the eyelashes. He looked like one of the Natives, a heathen who would stop at nothing simply because he had no fear of reprisals either from God or man.

Fear darkened her eyes; she was aware of throbbing pulse, of a sort of subconscious effort to steady her nerves. His thoughts appeared to be far away, distant from her and from his surroundings. Where was he? In England, perhaps with a wife or sweetheart he once had there? Sara's swift-winged thoughts brought her a picture of a beautiful doe-eyed Native girl with the figure of an angel.

She had to speak, to break the silence and to change the subject as well.

'Are the guides not coming back?'

'Muda and Tama?' He looked at her. 'They'll return in two weeks' time. By then you should be fit to make the river journey back to civilisation.'

'I'm to be here, then, with you, for at least two weeks?'

'Yes.'

'Your—wife—er—she won't care for me being here.' Sara had difficulty in phrasing the words. She wondered what he would say if he were to know that she had fallen in love with him.

But *was* it love? she was questioning herself the next moment. The powerful attraction and magnetic force which affected her emotions was palpable; the reaction to these, which she had assumed to be love, was of a nebulous character, which she now began to suspect was nothing more than desire of the flesh. For there was nothing deep or solid which she could grasp and say with confidence that this was love. Desire . . . Yes. His savage and violent approach had unquestionably awakened in her sensations which she had never experienced before, but then she had never found herself in such circumstances before, where the mysterious jungle was itself hauntingly compulsive, drugging the senses to a state where clear thought was not only difficult but almost impossible.

John was speaking, assuring her that his wife would not be jealous, if that was what Sara had meant.

She coloured and returned tartly,

'What I meant was that she might resent the intrusion of another person into her home!'

'As this doesn't happen to be her home,' he returned slowly, 'she couldn't possibly resent your presence here.'

'Not her home?' repeated Sara, puzzled. 'Where does she live then?'

John chose to ignore that, a circumstance that served to increase Sara's puzzlement. But she knew it would be fruitless to question him further. In any case, he was moving over to the cupboard on the wall from where he had taken the jar of ointment last night. This action reminding her of the sting, she enquired about it.

'It's better,' she was told brusquely. And after a short pause, 'I'm going to give you something to make you sleep. You're drugged against the pain, but it will wear off presently. As I can't give you that particular drug for another three hours, you'll take the sleeping pills.'

She stared uncomprehendingly.

'You have drugs—up here in this primitive part of the *ulu*?'

'Obviously I have drugs. Hasn't it dawned on you that, without drugs, you'd be writhing in pain?'

'Y—yes,' she returned wonderingly, 'yes, of course I would.'

She watched him at the cupboard, her face thoughtful. Those hands . . . long and slender and sensitive; his manner . . . certainly not a bedside one!—but certainly with the brisk and efficient quality of the professional. . . .

And he was in possession of drugs that could only have come up from Kuching, probably from the hospital there. Was he a doctor? The idea grew alongside the question as to why he had abandoned his profession to live like a Native. True, others had acted in a similar way, giving up a great deal in order to adopt a simple, trouble-free life.

Aware that she was assuming what might not be fact at all, Sara dismissed the matter from her mind and dwelt on her injuries, wondering if she would carry the scars for the rest of her life.

CHAPTER SEVEN

SARA had been reluctant to take the sleeping pills, half believing she would never waken again. But John had made her take them, and she had woken—woken to find that the pain was there, in her chest, in her shoulders and her back. One arm was heavily bandaged right down to the wrist, the other to the elbow. She wondered again if she was marked for life, feeling she would be exceptionally fortunate if in fact all the scars did fade. Managing to ease herself to a sitting position, she glanced around. Where had John slept? With his wife, in whatever place she lived? Sara doubted if he would leave her on her own all night, in case she wanted anything. Of course, he had given her the sleeping pills, and would know there was little possibility of her waking. All the same, she felt sure he would stay somewhere close. And she was right. He emerged from the other room, which was a small cookhouse of sorts because he had gone there for the water.

'Well, how are we this morning?' His voice, though brisk, held none of the harshness or animosity which had characterised it on those first meetings with him, nor did it carry the impatience she had noticed yesterday.

She looked at him, noticing particularly that he was immaculately clean, that he had shaved, that although his hair was fairly long it shone, and had been well brushed and combed.

'I think I feel a bit better, thank you,' she answered as he drew near to the bed.

'You have some considerable pain, though.' He stood silently weighing her up for a space, his features unsmiling and grim.

'Yes, I do have some pain. . . .' She paused, shades of anxiety in her eyes. 'There's something else, though, which has just come on—a sort of dizziness. I feel I'm about to pass out—lose consciousness.'

He drew a long breath and she was fearfully reminded of his remark about a fever.

'It's time for the pain-killer,' he said. 'But first your wounds must be dressed.'

Colouring instantly, she asked if there was some woman who could dress them.

'I prefer to do it myself,' she was told curtly. He walked over to a table in a dim corner of the hut and Sara realised that there was a tray on it, with some bottles, two small cardboard boxes and some bandages. There was a vacuum flask, from which he began to pour hot water.

'There must be a woman who can do it,' said Sara in some distress.

John turned around.

'I've already undressed you—At least, I removed the few shreds that were left after the bear had mauled you.'

Her colour deepened.

'That was different. I'd prefer one of the Native women——' She stopped, brought to silence by the look he gave her.

'Don't be such a damned fool! This is no time for modesty! You wouldn't be the first woman I've seen naked—nor the hundredth!'

'Hundredth?' she blinked, then nodded slowly. So she had been right. He *was* a doctor.

He came to her and flung aside the blanket.

'Oh, don't! There's no need——'

'We'll begin with the right arm; it took a bad mauling.' He was already undoing the bandage. With her free hand Sara reached for the blanket, but it was taken from her even as she touched it, and flung out of reach. She looked at him, but only for a second; she was curious to see her arm.

And she shut her eyes tightly when she did see it.

'God,' she whispered, 'it's—awful!'

'The scar will be with you a long time, I'm afraid.'

'You speak as if it'll go some time,' she said in surprise. 'I can't believe that.'

'It will certainly fade,' he assured her. He was working with speed and efficiency—no fumbling, no hesitation. The lotion from the bottle he had picked up was applied, then a clean bandage. The other arm was similarly attended to, and then came her chest, from where a large adhesive plaster was removed, swiftly, callously, in one deft movement of his hand. Sara's eyes closed under the pain. She looked down eventually, though, to see what damage had been done. One breast was badly clawed but, John said, the wounds had not gone very deep. The area between her breasts was raw, with blood oozing out, owing to the way he had ripped off the dressing. He cleaned it in the way he had cleaned the other wounds, and a new dressing was put on. Her hip was scraped; he examined it, his fingers probing, bringing the blood rushing to her face. She tried not to be conscious of his touch, of the contact of his flesh with hers, but despite her efforts emotions were being stimulated within her.

He ordered her to turn over, on to her stomach.

'Not too bad,' he said, his fingers moving over the scratches on her back. The bear had got her on the ground, she recalled, but she was rescued soon after that, so little damage had been done to her back—a few claw marks along her spine, and on the tops of her legs.

She was burning with embarrassment by the time he had finished with her, and to her chagrin he appeared to find some measure of amusement, as he gazed down into her hot face for a long moment before reaching for the blanket and covering her up.

'A modest female.' There was no mistaking the sneer in his voice, or the sarcasm. 'How very refreshing!'

She slid down, wincing with the pain it caused her.

'That remark,' she said, 'brands you a cynic.' He said

nothing and after a pause she added, 'Cynicism is usually the result of disillusionment.'

'Still trying?' with a fractional lift of his brows. 'Just you concentrate on getting well,' he advised, 'and forget all about the story you came here for.'

'I suppose you consider I've got only what I deserved?'

'No one,' he returned coldly, 'would wish another human being to be mauled by a wild animal.'

She averted her eyes, profoundly conscious of the censure in his tone.

'I shouldn't have said that,' she apologised. 'Please forgive me.'

He laid a hand on her forehead, and as before a frown knit his brow. She saw his eyes darken, his mouth take on a tighter line.

'I was right to decide you weren't fit to be moved,' he commented at last. 'You're in for a bout of fever.'

'Oh, no!' she cried. 'Not something else!' But the dizziness was more pronounced, and added to it was the sensation of burning within her. She had supposed this latter was the result of the ordeal through which she had passed, but now there was a drumming in her head, and a sort of throbbing in her chest. 'I ought to be in hospital. I'm a nuisance to you—and—and I c-can't h-help it——' The rising lump in her throat prevented her from finishing the sentence. She was crying quietly when, a moment later, she heard him say, curtly and yet not unkindly,

'You'll be as well looked after here as you would be in the hospital. But in any case, there's no way in which you could be taken there without serious risk of collapse. There aren't any roads, you know, and ambulances don't sail down rivers.'

The fever raged for three days, with Sara scarcely knowing where she was, and caring even less. She felt she must be very near to death, and there were several occasions when she would have welcomed it. On the fourth day, however, she was a little better, and by the end of the week she was able to appreciate the dawn, and the medley of sounds that came with it. From the fruit trees by the longhouse there appeared the inevitable succession of birds, heralding the fuller light that follows the first filtering rays of sunlight. The sweet liquid song of the bulbul mingled with the gay whispers of the sandpipers and the snatches of the magpie-robin's song. There was the cackle of the kingfisher and the occasional shriek of a kite, and various other, less noticeable, avian conversations. There could be heard the incessant chatter of monkeys, leaping from branch to branch like a troupe of trapeze artists. Sara could glimpse them from the open door of the hut.

She was still weak, and although she could sense the annoyance of the man whose guest she was, she did at the same time realise just how carefully he had tended her. But there were others who came and went, women with freshly-cooked rice biscuits or morsels of chicken and roast pig. It was Sri who came the most, though, to wash Sara and comb her hair, to change the blankets when they became wet with perspiration, which happened all the time for the first few days. She spoke not a word of English, so there was communication only when John translated for them. Sara came to like the Native girl enormously, finding her charmingly naïve, with an engaging personality and a deferential manner towards John, whose wife she seemed far too young to be. His behaviour towards her was a revelation to Sara, for he was gentleness itself, and it was plain that Sri adored him.

He said one day,

'You seem to like Sri?'

'I don't think anyone could dislike her,' she replied.
And then she ventured to ask how old she was.

'About fifteen.'

'Fifteen! But surely she oughtn't to be married.'

'Girls marry very young here.'

'You said—about. They never know exactly how old
they are, then?'

'Not up here, in the deep interior. Time means
nothing.'

'Don't these people ever want to change their way of
life?'

'Why should they? They're happy, contented with
what nature provides.'

Sara was surprised that he would talk to her like this,
but there had been a change, a very marked one. He was
far less antagonistic, but she supposed he could hardly
maintain his previous unfriendly manner when they were
so close, she living in his home and he sleeping—she felt
sure—in that other room which was the kitchen.

She asked, after a hesitant pause,

'How long have you been married, John?'

The glimmer of a smile touched his lips.

'You're very interested in my wife,' he said.

'Only because she seems so young—a mere child.'

'I haven't been married long enough to have tired of
it yet,' he told her, and the manner in which he said it
left Sara in no doubt that if she were to ask another
question she would meet with a snub.

The following morning she had been awake a mere five
minutes when he came in, wearing the loincloth. His hair
was wet and Sara realised he had been for a swim, for the

water droplets were on his chest as well, and clinging to the dark hairs on his legs.

'Have you been in the river?' she asked before he could speak.

'In a rock-pool,' he replied, coming over to her. 'Much better this morning,' he stated, taking her wrist in his fingers. 'But still a long way to go, I'm afraid. The fever's brought you down. This, on top of that attack and the injuries you sustained, has certainly weakened you, and I very much doubt if you'll be well enough to travel down-river to Kuching in just over a week's time.'

'Oh . . . please. . . .' She wanted only to get away, back to civilisation, to England. The assignment meant nothing any more; she was so depressed that the jungle had lost its attraction and she wished only to get away from it. The attack of that ferocious animal, then the fever—it was no wonder she wanted to get away, she thought, because if she didn't then something else might befall her. 'Please let me go!'

'You're so anxious to leave?'

'Of course I'm anxious to leave,' she answered pettishly. 'I've had more than enough of this place.'

'You came of your own accord,' he reminded her, and when she made no comment he went on, 'You've no further ambition, then, to get a story?'

She was sitting up in the bed, propped against some blankets that had been brought by Sri and folded to make a comfortable backrest. She had been staring at him, meeting his gaze, but she lowered her eyes when he asked the question, and was silent. For it had come to her that she *had* a story. Not the full one, but certainly enough information to form the basis for the kind of investigation that was bound to bear fruit. She knew, roughly, how long it was since he came up here; she knew he was a doctor. His first name was John. She had his description, knew he had an aristocratic background. She would have liked a few pictures, but that was not vitally important. Yes, she had a story . . . but would she publish it? What would her investigations reveal—should she decide to pursue them? Something detrimental to his character? No, she could have gambled all she owned that, whatever had brought him up here, it certainly was nothing disgraceful.

He moved, reminding her he was waiting for an answer to his question.

'I can't get anything from you,' she prevaricated, 'so ambition doesn't come into it.'

The grey eyes darkened with sudden suspicion.

'I don't care for your manner,' he told her bluntly. 'You journalists are just about the slyest bunch of scoundrels it's possible to meet, and I'd not be surprised if you embroidered what scant amount of information you've gained and produced the pack of lies your editor expects!'

Her eyes blazed.

'My editor expects the truth!'

'Can you honestly say,' he queried, his eyes mere slits beneath a scowling brow, 'that you've resigned yourself to failure?'

She coloured and glanced away, heard his swift, indrawn breath and said swiftly,

'I can't truthfully say whether I'm resigned to failure or not. I could write something, but I don't know if I shall.'

'A woman with a conscience?' he said cynically. 'And a journalist at that?' He shook his head. 'I'm not convinced, Sara.' He turned away to the kitchen where, she presumed, he was drying himself down with a towel. The idea brought other pictures, and questions. Did he go down to Kuching periodically? He had these medicines, which must have come from there; he had the tape recorder which used batteries; he had soap and towels and tinned food and several other commodities which the Natives did not have. If he did go down river to the capital then what did he wear?—Not the *chewat*, that was for sure!

He returned about half an hour later carrying a papier-mâché tray on which were a boiled egg and some packet toast.

'Thank you,' Sara murmured when he had placed the tray on the bed. 'You're—very kind to me.' Her eyes were wide, filled with gratitude, and for a long moment he stared right into them, an odd expression in his own. Then he turned away with such abruptness that the movement came as a shock.

'Before you leave here,' he said over his shoulder, 'I must have your solemn promise that you won't write the article—not one word about me.'

She stared at his gleaming, teak-coloured back. The mystery attached to him and his past still intrigued her and she felt sure that when she returned to England she would have to investigate. But she also felt that the investigation would be for her own satisfaction rather than for the production of the article.

'It's difficult to make a promise,' she told him frankly. 'You see, one's attitude changes, and although I might make that promise I could be tempted, one day, to go back on my word.'

He was shaking his head even before she had finished speaking.

'You're playing safe,' he said contemptuously. 'You don't want to make the promise because you know as well as I that once you've made it you definitely will not break it.' She said nothing and he turned, a tall forbidding figure with his long dark hair, his weather-bitten skin and those shrewd and penetrating eyes which at this moment were metal-hard. 'It's my opinion that you're undecided, mainly because you feel you owe me some- thing——'

'I owe you my life,' she broke in, and added that she owed him much more; she owed him gratitude for the care and attention he had given her during the time she had been here.

'If I thought that there was the least possibility of your writing about me for your newspaper, then I'd not hesitate to make sure you never reached England again,' he said, ignoring what she had been saying about gratitude. 'You see, I *have* suffered from the Press, as you suggested. I don't intend that it shall make me suffer again.'

Sara's eyes flickered with a new interest.

'Lies were written about you?' she ventured to ask, her breakfast forgotten.

'No, it was the truth.' A terrible bitterness entered his voice, but Sara's main impression was that he had become guarded . . . and that *he was lying* when he said the Press had written the truth about him! Why should he lie, though? She drew a breath, more baffled than ever. He said abruptly, glancing at the tray,

'Eat your egg. I'm allowing you up today.'

'Up?' Her eyes brightened. 'That'll be great!'

Her enthusiasm brought a faint smile to his lips, but he said,

'You'll want to get back to bed within minutes.'

'I don't think so,' she argued. 'I've been here much too long.'

'A week,' he reminded her. 'That's all.'

'It seems like a month,' she rejoined with a wry grimace.

He went out, returning later for the tray. He had changed into the khaki shorts and a faded blue shirt; his hair, though still wet, had been brushed and combed, and for the first time since she had met him he was wearing sandals—brown leather ones, well-worn, but still serviceable.

She had been up less than an hour when she asked to go back to bed. John had been outside the hut, reading beneath the shade of the tree, but he came the moment she spoke, and stood for a while frowning into her pale face and shaking his head slowly from side to side.

'I must send word down to Kuching and tell your two guides not to come back yet,' he decided. 'You'll be here for at least another fortnight.'

Sara sighed, but resigned herself to obeying his orders. After all, he was a doctor, so his decision must surely be the right one.

'Tama and Muda are students,' she said. 'They'll be due back at college shortly.'

'Yes, I know.' He paused in thought. 'In fact, if I'm not mistaken the college opens—after the present recess—in ten days' time.'

'You know?' She was being helped from the chair to the bed and, noticing John's eyes roving her nightgown-clad figure, she automatically drew her dressing-gown across the front of her body, bringing a rather sardonic quiver to his lips. She coloured, having to admit that modesty was out of place under the present circum-stances.

'Of course I know,' he answered, deciding to lift her

on to the bed. 'We're not totally out of touch up here.'

'But the Ubani Ulu are just about the remotest tribe of them all.' She was on the bed, every nerve quivering at the contact of his body as he lifted her. She was gently pushed down, and the blanket drawn up over her. She had not bothered to take off her dressing-gown and was glad that he had not insisted that she should do so. She could discard it later, when he was outside again, reading his book.

'We're remote, yes,' he agreed, but immediately went on to remind her that they did trade with the coast. 'And you managed to get up here,' he pointed out. 'So obviously we can get down to Kuching. It takes time, of course, but we have all the time in the world.' He continued by saying that she was wrong in assuming that the Ubani Ulu was among the very remotest of tribes. 'It's true that we're far into the interior of the jungle, but there are more remote tribes, and more primitive. The Punans, for example, are a very simple society, leading no settled existence at all.'

'They're nomads?'

'Yes; they wander about in small family groups through the dense, half-dark world of the deep tropical forest. They've no domestic animals; they don't grow rice—or in fact, anything at all.' He spoke generally, he said, but today there were exceptions.

'I thought that all tribes in Borneo engaged themselves in some kind of agriculture.' Sara was keeping the conversation going because she did not want him to leave the hut. He was so different, and his appearance was more attractive than ever to her. He had smiled; his voice and manner were friendly. Yes, she wanted to keep him with her, though what she hoped to gain she could not imagine.

'No, the majority of the Punans are hunters pure and simple. They erect temporary shelters—just a few large leaves supported on sticks, but they never stay long in any one place.'

'They find enough food, from the jungle?'

He nodded.

'They find various jungle fruits such as wild sago, and they kill various game with their primitive spears which are made of wood. Sometimes, though, they might get parangs from other tribes. They use the blowpipe, of course, as do the majority of the tribes here.'

'The blowpipe seems such an awkward weapon,' she said, thinking of the day she had seen him using one. 'They're so long, and they look heavy.'

'They're about eight feet long, but not too heavy at all.' He went on to tell her how the Punans, filling their cheeks with air, could make a poison dart go straight for about twenty yards; their aim was always unerring. He seemed to know so much about this primitive nomadic tribe that Sara found herself asking if he had ever lived with them, for she was recalling that Agan had told her boys that the white man had lived with several tribes before settling with the Ubani Ulu.

'Yes, I lived with them for a few months,' he replied. 'It was interesting. They're very mild savages, are never aggressively seeking trouble. They're generous to one another and are kind to their women—very different from some of the tribes here, who treat their women as slaves. The Punans seem surly when you first encounter them, but I very soon found them to be cheerful and happy.'

Sara was shaking her head.

'Happy . . . with so little,' she murmured, feeling that although civilisation had given so much to man, it had robbed him of much as well.

'Yes, Sara,' he said, a strange inflection in his tone, 'they're happy with so little.'

She looked at him.

'You are happy . . . with so little?' she had to say, watching his face closely in an endeavour to read his thoughts. For it was plain that he had given up a great deal when he decided to come here, into the jungle, to throw in his lot with peoples so very different from his own.

'I am happy, yes. . . .' But his eyes were far away, and his hands were clenched suddenly, as if he were affected by some strong emotional force which robbed him of some of his arrogance, took away some of the superiority and made him more human . . . and more vulnerable to hurt. The silence stretched, tense and profound, and somehow intimate. Sara thought of Sri and wondered how he could have married such a young child. And she wondered, too, if Sri satisfied him. Undoubtedly she could satisfy him in certain ways, but what of companionship, of the ability to·chat, to enter into discussions on various subjects? Sri was incapable of satisfying needs like those. It struck Sara that John must be a very lonely man, that he must spend long hours in this hut, which, though roomy, was little more than a hovel, made as it was from tree-trunks lashed together, with leaves of the nipa palm to form the roof. She glanced around, wondering—as she had wondered before—what was in the roughly-made locker type box on which stood an old Siamese jar, a lovely porcelain object which must be very valuable. Perhaps the locker contained books, perhaps private papers—or both.

John broke the silence at last, saying that he would be outside if she wanted him.

'Would you care for a book to read?' he asked.

'I did bring some with me,' she told him. 'They're in my rucksack.'

'Shall I pass it to you or would you like me to get a book out for you?'

'You can get it, please.' She watched him lift the large canvas bag and put it on a chair. She had suitcases, too, but had left them at the hotel in Kuching, for she knew she would need only rough clothes—denims and shirts— and a few underclothes. Unintentionally, she had left a couple of nightgowns out of the suitcases when she had had them taken from her room at the hotel by the porter. She found the nightgowns afterwards and had stuffed them into the rucksack, little knowing how glad she would be to have them.

The first thing that came to his hand was her notebook and she held her breath, aware that on the cover she had written, 'Only two shots up till now, but one's good. John killing wild pig with blowpipe.'

Sara watched his eyes fall to the words, saw the dramatic change come over his face. Slowly he turned, his features harsh, his eyes on fire.

'What is this——' He held out the notebook, tapping it with his fingers. 'You took a photograph—that day I killed the pig?'

She nodded dumbly, unable to find words. She felt ashamed, a traitor, and she could not blame him for the anger that looked out of his eyes, or the whip-like tone of his voice as he asked her where the camera was. And even as the question left his lips he was at the bag again, roughly tossing its contents on to the locker, intent on finding the camera and destroying the film at least.

'It isn't in there,' she said quickly, at which he demanded to know what she had done with it. She told him, since there was nothing else for it. If she had tried to deceive him she knew without any doubt at all that she would come off worst.

'You hid it, then showed yourself, and talked to me?' His voice had lost its cutting edge, but for Sara the contempt was even more effective in making her feel small and mean and utterly without principle.

'I'm sorry,' she muttered, aware of the inadequacy of the words but unable to find anything better.

His grey eyes were on her, dark and penetrating and filled with contempt.

'Sorry? Is that all you have to say?'

'I took it before—before all this——' She flung a hand expressively. 'I wouldn't take one now.'

The eyes flickered strangely.

'You wouldn't?'

She shook her head and said without hesitation,

'No, John, I wouldn't.'

'Why?' He looked from her to the book he held; she saw him read the words again. 'I asked you why?' he repeated when she made no answer.

'Things are—are different.'

'In what way?'

What was this? A cross-examination?

'I owe you so much,' she answered, looking at him with shadowed eyes. 'It would be a rotten way to repay you for all you've done for me this past week.'

A silence followed, tense and profound like the one that had gone before. Sara's pulse quickened for no apparent reason; her nerves were taut, her mind confused. For it did seem that John was relieved by her admission that it would be rotten of her to repay his goodness by taking pictures of him. Did it mean that he wanted to regard her in a different light from that in which he had regarded her before? Her breath caught at the idea, and a sort of quiet joy entered her heart.

Then suddenly she was remembering Sri, the lovely Native girl who was John's wife. . . .

'I'll find the camera,' he was saying tersely, and the next moment Sara was staring at his back as he strode to the open door. 'You can keep the camera,' he promised, 'but I want all the films you have.'

He was gone before he had finished speaking, and a few minutes later Sri came in, a shy smile on her dusky face. She had some rice biscuits in her hand, and in the other hand a rough earthenware mug in which were pieces of wild mango. Sara accepted both the biscuits and the fruit graciously, giving Sri a smile and saying thank you, aware that by now the Native girl knew what that meant. In any case, John had, during the past day or two, been translating rather more than usual, and he had taught Sri a fair number of English words. Sara disliked the mango fruit, but she ate it, rewarded by the bright smile she received from the girl who, squatting on the floor, was watching Sara intently. What a pity they could not converse, thought Sara with a little sigh. She would have liked to question Sri about her marriage, ask her how long she had been John's wife, but it was impossible. She did venture to say the one word, 'Linjau,' however, and Sri's eyes lit up and she said awkwardly,

'Good—*dayong*. . . .'

'*Dayong?*' repeated Sara slowly.

Sri's lips parted in a smile. She nodded vigorously, delighted by Sara's repetition. It was plain that she thought Sara knew what it meant.

'*Dayong!* Linjau!'

What did it mean? It was no use trying to get anything

from Sri, so Sara decided to ask John what it meant, which she did, immediately on his return.

'What does *dayong* mean?'

'Medicine-m——' He stopped abruptly. 'Why do you want to know?' he demanded forcefully. 'Where have you heard the word?'

Medicine-man. . . . So the tribe knew John was a doctor. Had he treated any of them? Sara felt he would have to be extremely careful, since it would be so easy to offend the Native medicine-man.

'I asked you a question!' John had tossed down the camera close to the rucksack; the film had been taken out and was in his hand. 'Answer me!' Imperious the order. Sara's chin tilted and a sparkle lit her eye.

'Don't speak to me like that,' she began, when he interrupted her, saying roughly,

'Sri came in here when I'd gone out. Have you been talking to her?'

'How could I talk to someone who doesn't understand my language?'

He strode to the door and called loudly,

'Sri!'

The girl came at once, not having been far away at all.

He spoke to her and Sara watched the girl's expression as she answered what was obviously a question. Sara understood one word only: *dayong*. John flicked a hand, indicating that Sri should leave the hut, which she did, immediately.

'So you tried to pump her, eh?' he said unpleasantly.

'It became obvious to me that you are a doctor,' she returned quietly. 'The way you dressed the wounds; the manner of your examination—Oh, and several other pointers. I guessed you must be a doctor——' Her glance fell to his hands. 'I think you're a surgeon,' she said, and knew by his expression that she had hit on the truth. He said nothing, though, and after a slight hesitation she added, 'The reason why you're up here has something to do with your profession——'

'Shut up!' he broke in harshly. 'You know nothing at all about it! Already you're guessing, concocting a story, reaching conclusions that——'

'You were struck off?' Sara could not have said how words like that came to leave her lips. The thought had come; indeed it was the only logical idea that could possibly have emerged, but she would never have believed herself capable of voicing something that should obviously have been kept to herself. She saw his face twist, saw the sheer venom that looked out from his eyes. Fear entered into her and she shrank further down beneath the blanket. He could kill her and get away with it. She had died of the fever, he would say. He'd be believed simply because all these Natives knew she had had the fever, and in any case, they thought so much about him that Sara was sure they would lie if necessary, to save him from harm.

He came close to the bed and stood over her, a tall, menacing figure, his nostrils flaring, a murderous expression on his face.

'You're not leaving here until I feel absolutely sure that you'll not write one single word about what you've seen or heard up here. Do you get me?' he added with a snarl.

She looked up at him, her face white, her whole body trembling.

'I'll make the promise here and now,' she answered. 'I give you my solemn word not to write anything at all about you.'

'Your editor—he'll want to know what you've been doing with your time.'

'I shall tell him about the attack, and the fever. If I go home immediately you say I'm fit to travel then there won't be much time to account for. He knows how long and unpredictable the river travel is. I can easily convince him that I had no time to do any investigating.'

'I wonder if I can trust you?' His eyes, having lost their fire, were subjecting her to a cold, speculative look. 'I ought not to trust a woman, especially one who's a member of the Press.'

'You can trust me,' she assured him quietly. 'I shan't go back on my word.'

He continued to look at her for a long moment, and then to her relief his face cleared and he uttered a faint sigh, saying levelly,

'I accept your word, but if you let me down then I assure you you'll regret it.'

Was it a threat? Surely he would not come to England just to punish her, should she go back on her word. And yet, looking up into that stern, incalculable countenance, Sara felt there was nothing she would put past him.

He took the film into the other room and came back without it. She watched him begin to put the camera in the rucksack, then stop and turn.

'You have other cameras?' His voice was cold, his gaze one of steely intentness.

She nodded.

'One small one. It's in the rucksack.'

He searched for it, his profile grim. The camera was brought out, opened, and the film removed. After that he proceeded to empty the bag, found several films and confiscated them all. Sara said as he began to replace her belongings in the bag.

'There was no need to do that. I wouldn't have taken any more pictures.'

'I'd rather be sure that it's impossible for you to do so,' he said brusquely.

'You've just said you accepted my word,' Sara reminded him.

'As far as the story. I do take your word about that. But you could still have taken pictures.'

'Well, I wouldn't have done. What good would they be to me if I did?' He made no answer, and a few minutes later he went outside again and settled down with his book.

CHAPTER EIGHT

JUST as John had predicted, it was another fortnight before he could pronounce her fit to travel down-river to the capital. But the two Dyak boys could not come for her. They sent word that they had to be back at college, and to Sara's amazement John offered to accompany her to the coast, from where she could get the regular sea transport to Kuching.

'It's going to inconvenience you,' protested Sara, her feelings mixed. On the one hand the idea of spending three days in his company was undoubtedly attractive, but on the other hand she was acutely conscious of the danger involved, since they would have to camp at night. Moreover, there was the thought of his wife, who would surely hate the idea of his going off like that, with another woman, for three days and nights. And finally there was the thought that, the way she was feeling at present, Sara was quite likely to be affected by his attractions to the point where she could suffer severe heartache when the final parting took place.

Three days in the lonely jungle, gliding down rivers in a small boat. Nothing to do but talk. . . . And the nights. . . . She would probably sleep in the boat, while he would make himself a rough shelter on the bank. There would be meals prepared and eaten together. It was all too intimate, she decided, but her protest had met with a shrug and the logical statement that she could scarcely make the journey on her own.

'As for inconvenience—well, I've all the time I need. I shall probably enjoy it.'

She glanced warily at him.

'I don't know . . . you see——'

'I shan't attempt to molest you,' he assured her. 'That was then and this is now. It's different.'

'Different?' she repeated swiftly, looking into his eyes and noticing that his expression was closed. 'In what way is it different?'

'It's of no importance,' he answered non-committally. 'As I said, you'll be quite safe.'

She said,

'Sri—your wife—won't she mind?'

'Sri doesn't know what it is to be jealous,' he replied with a shake of his head.

'She's very sweet. I'll feel a little sad at saying goodbye to her.'

'She is very sweet, I agree. And she's taken to you. I expect she'll feel sad, too, at saying goodbye.' He was looking at her strangely, and there was something about his tone that was almost regretful. Sara, a tingling sensation in the region of her spine, regarded him with a puzzled expression. Could it be that *he* would feel a certain amount of sadness at the parting——? She cut her thoughts abruptly, telling herself that such an idea was absurd. He would be relieved to see the back of her, and she firmly believed that he never wanted to set eyes on her again.   .

She and he were in the garden he had made surrounding the hut, a pretty little garden with allamandas and gloriosas and amaryllis flourishing among bougainvillaea vines and hibiscus bushes. As there were no well-defined seasons in this part of the world flowers and trees flaunted their beauty the whole year round, thriving in the humid, hothouse conditions of hot sun and abundant water. The earth was smelling freshly of rain, for during the night the heavens had opened and for several hours a tropical storm had raged.

Although she had been up and about for almost two weeks Sara was still living in the hut where, said John, he could keep an eye on her.

'In any case, you couldn't have slept in a tent now that your boys aren't with you,' he had added. And he had deliberately avoided her gaze when she suggested that she live in the longhouse. 'There isn't room,' he had told her. And in any case, Penghulu Mira was still not pleased at her disobedience, even though nothing calamitous had occurred as a result of her upsetting the omen birds.

During all this time Sara had been exceedingly puzzled about the relationship between John and his young wife. For one thing Sri never shared a meal with him, and although never a day passed without her coming to the hut, she never stayed long. Sara learned that she lived with her parents and brothers and sisters in one of the doors of the longhouse, and one day Sara had ventured to ask if this state of affairs was usual among the Natives.

John had shrugged and passed off the question in a manner which seemed far too casual to be sincere.

'In some cases, yes,' and he had immediately changed the subject and Sara had never had the temerity to mention it again. But it was natural that she should begin to wonder if John ever visited his wife at night. Sara knew that much went on on the verandah between the boys and girls of the tribe, who would share a 'mat' for the night, but try as she might she could not visualise John doing a thing like that, despite his primitive and savage approach towards herself.

But if he never visited the Native girl, then what was the reason for the marriage?

It was all so baffling, but at the same time Sara reminded herself that it was no business of hers.

It was arranged that she and John should set off on the Saturday morning early—if no rain occurred during the previous night, for then the rivers would be in spate. Sara's feelings were very mixed. She had grown to love the jungle in spite of the mauling from the honey-bear, and of what she had said as a result. More herself now, she was able again to appreciate all that prodigal nature was supplying up here, in this tropical jungle where civilisation had scarcely encroached, where the people were friendly and kind, living the simple life, away from all cares, away from such things as artificial pleasures and their futility of purpose, away from the bickering absurdities which affected not only people but nations. Here, they were ignorant of such things, and although they were obviously deprived, the compensations more than made up for what they were missing.

At least, so it was in Sara's opinion, and she had more than once—in her conversations with John—admitted it, surprising him at first, but later he had become used to the idea that she was appreciative of her surroundings, and she noticed that he was strangely affected in a way that left him in a silent, brooding frame of mind. He would become remote from her, and from his surroundings, as if he were being drawn deeply into some idea which absorbed his entire mind—but which, eventually, he rejected.

John had a *prahu*, and for the whole of the Friday he was occupied in doing some work on it, most of which seemed to be concerned with the outboard motor. Sara, dressed in an orchid blue linen blouse and tight denims several shades darker, looked young and unsophisticated as she stood there by the river bank, watching him. She was still pale, and her right arm was bandaged, but in the main she was herself again, and several times she noticed that John would straighten up from his task and his grey eyes would flicker over her slender figure before coming to rest for a brief and unfathomable moment on her face.

'Have you got everything ready?' he was asking her later, when they were having their evening meal of roast wild pig which he had killed the day before. 'We want to start very early in the morning—as soon as it's light, in fact.'

Which was about a quarter past six, she knew, since there was no real dawn here. It was dark at six o'clock in the morning and broad daylight fifteen minutes later.

'Yes, I have everything ready,' she replied, and something in her tone brought the swift enquiry, as John paused in his eating,

'You don't sound altogether happy at the idea of leaving here.'

'I have to go,' she said, and again her voice was flat.

'That,' he said with a faint lift of his brow, 'is not an answer to my question.'

She looked at him, at the attractive way he had done his hair, brushing it back from his temples but unable to keep the wave from falling on to his forehead. So tawny his skin! And with that long dark hair. . . . This evening he was dressed in a checked shirt and a pair of corduroys held up with a leather belt. The shirt was open to reveal the bronzed throat and chest. Civilised clothes . . . but the heathen was there. Sara's breath caught as he smiled; she felt as if her heart was receiving every drop of blood in her body. Nerves tingled, emotion flared. She had questioned her feelings for him, unsure of whether it were love she felt, or merely desire for that sinewed, pagan body. Desire was still there, but she knew now that love had come to her and was growing all the time.

The sooner she was away from him the better, for even if he had not been married already he was still unreachable, he and she a world apart.

He gave a slight cough, reminding her that he was expecting her to say something in response to his comment.

'I'm not exactly over the moon about leaving,' she said, and tried to make her voice sound light. 'I feel I've not had an opportunity of enjoying what the jungle has to offer.'

'You obviously feel it has much to offer?' John picked up a piece of meat with his fork and put it into his mouth. 'Most people would hate it—the heat, the humidity, the violent thunderstorms—We can have as many as two hundred and fifty a year, and although they come mainly at night it's impossible to ignore them.' He looked at her, waiting, as if he were more than ordinarily interested in her response.

'I know all that, John. I've been here a few weeks, remember. There are disadvantages, yes, but look at the compensations. I now take back the criticism I made at first when I said I didn't know how you could put up with it—the primitive way of living, I mean.'

The grey eyes were narrowed, intent as he said,

'Would you like to make your life up here, Sara?'

Sudden confusion brought delectable colour to her cheeks. What was he saying?—or perhaps 'offering' was a more appropriate word? He had a lovely Native wife . . . but these men of the primitive tribes could take more than one wife. Her colour deepened; her voice was sharper than she intended as she replied.

'No—no, I wouldn't care to live up here permanently!'

'I didn't think you would.' The tenseness had gone from the atmosphere; he was smilingly indifferent as he looked at her and said, 'It's no place for a white woman anyway. It would only be an eccentric who would forsake the so-called good life and come up here to settle.'

'Has any white woman settled up here?' she asked involuntarily, and he laughed.

'If she has, it would be a long time ago—and I expect she very soon lost her head.'

'You once told me you'd like to see my head dangling on a piece of string,' she could not resist reminding him.

The smile that had lingered after the laugh faded instantly.

'That was then and this is now,' he said. 'No, you're too beautiful, Sara, for me to wish you any harm.'

She swallowed hard, for suddenly her throat felt dry.

'You've said that twice, John—the thing a-about then and—and now. I asked you what you meant but you wouldn't tell me?' What was she pleading for—a declaration of love? No! There was Sri, the lovely, gentle Native girl who quite plainly adored him.

John was frowning and Sara realised at once that he was regretting the trend which the conversation was taking; he was vexed with himself for repeating those cryptic words which inevitably must puzzle his companion.

He changed the subject abruptly and from then on the conversation was concerned only with the journey down to the coast.

It was soon after they had finished the meal that Sri arrived, which was unusual, since she had never come so late before—at least, not since Sara was up and capable of doing things for herself. Before that Sri had come in to make Sara comfortable for the night. John and Sara were both busy, John in the kitchen preparing food and flasks, and Sara packing the last few of her belongings into the rucksack.

'Linjau. . . .' Sri's eyes were filled with tears and Sara's heart caught because she was sure that it was Linjau's forthcoming absence that was causing the girl distress.

Sara pointed and Sri went into the other room. She was soon pouring out some story, in between sobs. Sara heard John's soothing voice and knew he had the girl in his arms. What was the matter? Sara felt deeply anxious, wishing there was someone else who could take her to the coast.

After about ten minutes or so John and Sri emerged, and to Sara's astonishment the girl was smiling happily, her tears having ceased miraculously. In John's hand was a handkerchief. . . .

How gentle he always was with Sri! Sara half envied her, and yet she was deeply sorry for her, because although John seemed to think a great deal about her, Sara could not for one moment imagine his being in love with her. They were so different; he was an educated man of culture, a doctor, while she was a simple Native child, unable even to speak his language. Sara frowned as she looked from one to the other; John's action in marrying her was unfathomable, completely baffling. Yet he had married her, and both he and Sri seemed quite happy, each in their own way.

Sri smiled at Sara and said softly,

'*Salamit*, Sara.'

'*Salamit*, Sri—good night and sleep well.'

Sara could not help asking John what had been wrong with Sri, although she half expected he would evade an answer. To her surprise he explained that Sri had been upset by a private matter, which she had brought to him, hoping he could sort it out for her.

'It means,' added John finally, 'that I shall have to carry on to Kuching instead of leaving you at the coast and coming straight back.'

'You'll be staying in Kuching—at an hotel?'

He had not told her what Sri's trouble was, but he seemed optimistic about managing to put it right for her.

'Yes, I shall have to stay,' he replied. 'I wouldn't be able to arrive there and leave on the same day.'

Sara's eyes flickered over him, taking in the shirt and the corduroys, both of which were a big improvement on what he had worn before, even the shorts and the shirt. But it was not the attire for an hotel. . . .

What would he wear, then? It had already dawned on Sara that he must possess other wearing apparel, and she was exceedingly interested in the transformation which must inevitably be brought about when he was attired in proper clothes.

The sun was just up when they sailed away in John's *prahu*, John having to punt and pole along the narrow river, but when they reached a wider stream he would be able to use the outboard motor. They came to a longhouse some hours later and he pulled in, mooring the *prahu*, then helping Sara out on to the path, which was made of tree trunks laid upon the ground. The *tua rumah* appeared at once—not anyone Sara recognised from the upstream journey because John had decided to travel only part way along the Kalui River, and then take to the Batang Atung, which was a smaller river but not so hazardous as to the number of rapids they would have to negotiate. Sara had been greatly puzzled by the fact that he had attached the word *batang* to the river—and to others he had mentioned—and she asked him if the word had two meanings.

'Tama and Muda called the fallen trees we saw *batangs*,' she ended with an edge of bewilderment to her voice.

'Yes, the word does have two meanings,' John told her. 'It means river, but your guides were quite right: it also means a fallen tree.'

The *tua rumah* was obviously pleased to see John, who spoke to him in fluent Malay, then introduced him to Sara. The man, Abit Nuran, could speak sufficient English to be able to make Sara welcome in words she could understand. She and John were led up the notched log on to the verandah, and she saw the familiar pattern of doors, with the miscellany of embellishments around or above them. There were shields and gongs and parangs, and the inevitable trophies, hideous skulls older than the *tua rumah* by far, and close beside one of these Sara noticed a pronged skewer holding small pieces of pig-meat, and a cup made from bamboo in which—she assumed—was a small quantity of *borak*. Food and drink for the sacred skull. . . .

They were given rice biscuits and *borak* by one of the chief's wives who, dressed in a gay sarong, went back afterwards to her task of pounding rice in a heavy wooden mortar, while curious-eyed brown children, quite naked, stood around, watching the two white-skinned people with silent intentness. But it was Sara who attracted most attention, since John was well known to everyone. The *tua rumah* said something to John, pointed to Sara, then laughed.

'What is he saying?' Sara wanted to know.

'He asks if we've lain together——'

'Oh!—and doesn't he know about Sri?' she queried tartly.

'Sri. . . .' The name was repeated by the chief, and brought a sudden frown to his face at the same time.

'Yes, he knows all about Sri,' answered John, obviously amused about something. The chief repeated the Native girl's name again, apparently asking John a question about her. He answered and the frown cleared from the *tua rumah*'s forehead.

Not long afterwards Sara and John were on their way again, and she asked him about some beautiful porcelain she had noticed. It was thick with dust but seemed to be in perfect condition otherwise.

'It looks very valuable,' she added. 'I saw similar things in other longhouses, when we were coming up.'

'Those you saw just now are extremely valuable. There was Sung and Ming, Kanghsi and Chienlung. They all came here, long ago, brought by the Chinese who traded with the jungle tribes, taking the produce supplied by the Natives in exchange for this exquisite pottery. The Natives consider these vases and jars to be sacred, passing them down from generation to generation, and there'd be murder for anyone who dared to try to steal any of them.'

'You have a Ming plaque, and an old Siamese jar, I noticed.'

He nodded, his eyes on the rapids ahead.

'Gifts,' he returned briefly.

'For something—er—special?' She was making a guess, suspecting he had used his knowledge and experience in saving someone's life perhaps.

'I shall have to concentrate on these. . . .' He was getting ready to use extra exertion in poling. Sara felt a stab of vexation at the subtle manner in which he had avoided answering her question. She watched his powerful manoeuvring of the vessel as he brought it safely across the rapids, then paddled it away from a swift current with incredible ease and skill. He had it in the concave side of the bend, where the lesser current prevailed, so that the *prahu* was taking an almost straight course instead of following the pattern of the river. He seemed to be thoroughly at home and confident, and even when they met a really dangerous part of the river he managed the rapids with almost the same ease as before.

Sara felt so safe, and exhilarated too, because this journey was something she would remember, something she would never experience again as long as she lived.

That night they stayed in a longhouse. It stood on the bank by a great clump of trees which John had pointed out to Sara, telling her that they would be welcomed by

his friend, Lawi Bengar, the village chief. He steered the
prahu towards the jetty, which was made of a number of
batangs roped together. The longhouse was raised on stilts
as usual, for the river often flooded over its banks and
always there were swamps as a result. Pigs grunted
beneath the slatted floor of the verandah, and sturdy
fighting-cocks crowed by several of the doors. A feast was
provided in John's honour, and again the chief spoke
and pointed to Sara who, this time, refrained from asking
what the Native had said. John was amused as before, so
that was enough to stem any questions.

She coloured and saw him look at her strangely,
thought he drew a faint sigh but could not be sure. But
during the long day they had been together she had
several times felt that they were close, in comradeship
and harmony, and the vague idea did come to her that
he might be feeling regret that he was married. Yet this
was a fanciful thought, as nothing could come of this
relationship even if he were free. Sara had been into this
before and reached the same decision. If only she and
John had met in ordinary circumstances . . . if he had
never come up here then she would not have come either.
. . . So many ifs and adding up to nothing in the end,
simply because if he and she had not met up here they
would never have met at all. She often wondered why he
had been struck off the register—*if* he had been struck
off, and she felt almost sure he had. She had previously
decided that he had done nothing disgraceful, but doctors
were not struck off unless they had committed some
serious offence. She frowned and thrust the matter from
her mind, just as she had done several times before. She
could not bear to think of him doing something so wrong
that he was barred from following his chosen profession.

The feast consisted of chicken, rice and pork soup,

everyone helping themselves to this latter, for which a rough wooden ladle was provided.

'*Banyak sedap*,' said the chief, smiling at Sara through paper-dry lips and showing long black teeth with gaps between. He was gnarled and wrinkled, with hornbill earrings and tattoo marks on his chest and arms. Some of the Native men wore loincloths made of thin bark from trees, and had large numbers of bracelets round their legs.

'He means,' John was saying in explanation of the *tua rumah*'s words, 'that the food was very tasty.'

'Oh . . . tell him yes, it was delicious.'

John obligingly translated for her; the chief sent her another smile, then said something to John, who began to shake his head, then stopped, a slight frown creasing his dark forehead.

'I'm afraid, Sara,' he said with a sort of amused apology, 'that we shall have to share a room for the night.'

Startled, she jerked him a glance.

'What—why——?'

'You know how it is,' he broke in chidingly, 'so don't put on the pretence. Lawi Bengar expects us to lie together. The desire must be satisfied or the omen birds will be offended.'

Was he suppressing laughter? wondered Sara, glancing suspiciously at him. His face was a mask, unreadable. It was the chief who seemed to be all agog, waiting for her to say something. But what was she supposed to say? She swallowed the dryness in her throat and managed a smile as she told John that they ought not to have stayed here tonight. He turned to the chief and spoke in the Malay tongue. The chief was obviously pleased by what he heard and Sara, her heart beating overrate, wondered what he would do were she to get up from this squatting position she was in on the mat they had provided, and make a run for it.

Not that she was entertaining for one moment the idea of anything so foolhardy. Her recent experience with the honey-bear was more than enough to keep her from venturing alone in the jungle again, in spite of John's assurance that the honey-bear very rarely ventured out in the way that one had done. Nevertheless, although his assurance had been given, he did advise her to be wary in future.

'I've told the chief that you're willing,' said John with a trace of mocking amusement. 'I know you didn't say you were,' he added rather quickly when she seemed ready with a denial, 'but he expected you to be willing.'

She drew a breath. Once they were in the room she would tell him to go and find somewhere else to sleep!

One of the chief's daughters came forward shyly and said,

'*Bilek*,' and added something as she raised a hand as an indication that Sara would follow her.

'*Bilek* means a room, an apartment,' explained John who, standing up, was saying goodnight to his friend and within seconds of Sara's entering the room he was with her, closing the door behind him.

'You can't stay here,' she began, when the lifting of an eyebrow stopped her.

'My dear Sara,' he said with some amusement, 'we've been living intimately for almost three weeks. Another night won't make much difference—You're very lovely when you blush,' he added softly, moving towards her and reaching out to take her hand. 'What do you want me to do, child? I can't go from here because Lawi Bengar's still on the verandah, and will be for hours yet. And even then there'll be others there, sleeping outside their doors, on the mats.'

'We haven't shared a room,' Sara reminded him. 'Living intimately, as you term it, occurred when I was ill. You slept in your kitchen, I believe?'

'Yes,' he agreed, 'I did. But that was different. We shall have to share, I'm afraid.' He looked at the hand he held, and a faint sigh escaped him. He released it and glanced around. There was a bed made from bamboo poles with a mattress of palm leaves forming the base. Two brightly-coloured blankets had been provided and little else. There was a box-like chair, and a chest-like piece of furniture with at one end a protruding board, shaped and painted like a child's head, but it was very crudely done and the upright ears seemed more suited to a jungle cat than a child. Sara frowned as she examined it and asked John what it was. There followed a long and undecided hesitation before John spoke, and when he did speak it was to say, slowly and reluctantly,

'It's a sarcophagus . . . of a young child——'

'A sarcophagus!' she repeated, shuddering and backing away, her eyes wide and disbelieving. 'Are—are you s-sure?'

He nodded his head.

'It wasn't always in here,' he said thoughtfully. 'The last time I saw it it was on the verandah, against the partition wall right at the end.' He looked at her with an expression half amused, half serious. 'I didn't know whether to tell you or not, but thought it best to, just in case you should let your curiosity get the better of you and take a peep inside. The lid's not fixed down, you see.'

She went pale.

'The—the body of—of a child is in—there?'

'Of course. That's what a sarcophagus is—a coffin.'

She swallowed, and stared, wondering how she was

going to get any sleep, knowing that a child's body was there in that crudely-made coffin.

'I can't—can't sleep in here, John! Why have they put it here—when you said it was on the verandah before?'

He shrugged his shoulders.

'That's something I can't answer, Sara. It could be that they feel it's safer here, or warmer——'

'Warmer!' she echoed. 'A corpse—to be kept warm!'

'Why do you suppose they light fires beneath the skulls? It's to keep them warm. There's a great emphasis on death here,' he went on, 'and the dead must be cared for, otherwise they might be angry and mete out some bad luck.'

She drew a breath. This was one of the beliefs of these Natives and she had to accept it. But she said again that she could not sleep in the room. John eventually persuaded her that the chief had probably thought he was honouring her by putting her in here with his young son— oh yes, he said, it was the chief's son by his fifth, and very young, wife.

'As I say, he probably is honouring you, and to leave and sleep on the verandah would be such a great insult that I couldn't be responsible for the consequences.'

Sara looked at him suspiciously, but she knew by his expression that he was not deceiving her.

'So I've got to sleep here,' she sighed, taking another step to lengthen the distance between her and the coffin.

'I'm with you, and I promise not to molest you,' he reminded her quietly, and she found herself nodding, profoundly grateful for his company.

The following morning they were off early, after making gifts of cloth for sarongs, tobacco, and sweets for the children.

'You keep a stock of these things?' Sara said, for John had made gifts at the other longhouse earlier in the day.

'Yes. I usually stock up each time I go to Kuching.'

'You go often?'

'Not often, but regularly.'

'So many times a year?'

'Fishing, Sara?'

She shook her head.

'I gave you my promise, John. I would never let you down.' She looked earnestly into his eyes, saw them flicker, then he looked away and this time she definitely did hear the small sigh that escaped him.

'I go four times a year,' he told her, his eyes now on the river. It was widening out, so the motor could be used for a while. Later, though, their way was along a much smaller stream and once again he would have to resort to his own strength to get them through. They came to rapids several times, and on one occasion they were so treacherous that Natives tending a padi field came to John's aid. Everything was taken from the *prahu* by these grinning, husky men who, because they were nearer to the coast than the more primitive tribes of the far interior, seemed more civilized, wearing shorts for one thing, and only a few wore earrings and bangles. While they were getting the boat over the rapids Sara was taking a precarious walk through a winding rocky path which was so slippery that she almost fell on her face several times. The *prahu* was soon on its way again, though, and from then on the passage seemed easy.

That night they camped, John in a rough shelter made from poles and leaves of the nipa palm for a covering, and Sara in the boat. The previous night John had slept on the floor, taking one of the blankets, while Sara had occupied the bed. He had promised that they would not

stay in a longhouse again and she was grateful, thanking
him and blushing at the same time. There had been no
privacy for either of them, and she thought that perhaps
he was thinking of himself as well as her when he made
the decision to camp.

CHAPTER NINE

SARA bathed and changed, putting on a pretty flowered
cotton dress, one of the many she had left behind in the
hotel at Kuching. She and John had arrived less than an
hour ago and he had booked in at the same hotel, going
off immediately to the room allocated to him. The hotel
manager greeted him like an old friend, taking not a bit
of notice of John's long hair or rather grimy clothes. He
had brought a leather suitcase with him on the *prahu,* and
this was carried away by the hotel porter. John had said
they would go out during the afternoon, as he wanted to
take her to the hospital. But first they would have lunch
in the hotel.

She came down from her room and entered the lounge.
John was already there and as he had not noticed her she
stood for a moment, an involuntary gasp escaping her at
the dramatic transformation in his appearance. He was
dressed casually but immaculately in a pair of pearl-grey
linen slacks, a draped-line jacket over a gleaming white
shirt, and a dark blue tie. His hair was still long, brushed
back from his forehead, with the inevitable wave falling
on to it, as it always did. Rising when he saw her, he
smiled as his eyes flickered over her, and there was an
odd inflection in his voice as he said,

'You look charming, Sara. Sit down and I'll order you a drink.'

She thanked him shyly for the compliment and had to say, hoping she was not speaking out of turn,

'You look very different, too, John. There's quite a transformation!'

To her relief he laughed.

'I must admit,' he returned, 'that it's rather good to get back to civilisation now and then.' He beckoned to the waiter, who came at once and spoke in English.

'What can I do for you, sir?'

John asked Sara what she was having, then gave the order. His own drink was on the table before him. Sara, reflecting on the fact that the hotel manager—who had been in the lobby when they arrived—had known John, asked if the waiter knew him too.

He shook his head.

'He's new since I was here last.' There was a slight pause before he added, avoiding her fixed gaze, 'You're bound to discover my name, now that we're here, so I might as well tell you: it's Parker.'

'Parker. . . .' She repeated it slowly, thinking furiously, endeavouring to place a John Parker, to recall anything she had ever read about the disappearance of a surgeon of that name. There was nothing, not even the merest thread of memory. His disappearance was about the same time as she had started with the *Sunday Sphere*—or perhaps it had occurred a short while before. Sara knew she could find out all about John Parker when she got back to England . . . if she wanted to, that was, and she rather thought that once she and he parted, here in Kuching, her wisest course would be to forget all about him.

'If you're ready,' he was saying when they had finished their drinks, 'we can go into the restaurant and have lunch. I've telephoned the hospital and they're expecting us at three o'clock.'

Something in his tone impelled her to ask if he was well known at the hospital.

'I feel you must be,' she added, thinking of the medical supplies he had in his hut.

'Yes, they do know me,' was all he said, rising from his chair and glancing towards the archway leading to the restaurant.

They sat at a window table and ate 'rat' noodles, which were made from chopped beef which, explained John when on reading the menu Sara had made a wry mouth, resembled the flesh of a rat. Following these they were served with crab claws and sliced cold duck. Iced beer was brought for John at his request, while Sara drank refreshing lemonade.

Coffee was served in the lounge, Sara having *kopi-hsi*—coffee with milk, and John the black coffee—*kopi-o*.

He took her by taxi to the hospital, saying they could enquire, on the way back, about a flight for her.

'I expect you want to leave as soon as possible?' He turned from her as he spoke, staring through the window of the taxi. Sara was frowning, thinking that by this time tomorrow she and John could have said goodbye. . . .

'I—er. . . .' She tailed off slowly and he turned with a sharp gesture to examine her expression. She was biting her underlip, confusion bringing colour to her cheeks.

'You don't want to leave yet.' It was a statement; she had expected him to say something of the kind. She nodded and replied frankly,

'I'd like to stay a little while—not long, because Joe will expect me back once I've sent the cable to let him know I'm back in Kuching.'

'You've not sent the cable yet?'

'No. I could have done, from the hotel, but—but. . . .'
Again her voice trailed and she averted her head, hiding
her expression. Taking her by surprise, he tilted her chin
with his finger, and although she could have twisted
away she refrained, obeying his silent command instead,
and meeting his penetrating gaze. Her mouth quivered
and before she knew it his lips were touching it, gently,
caressingly . . . so very different from the savage approach of a few weeks ago.

Was he falling in love with her? The thought was
crucifying simply because of the existence of his wife, a
gentle doe-eyed creature who must be eagerly awaiting
his return to the primitive jungle that was the only home
she had ever known.

He drew away, his eyes darkly brooding. And then it
was only his profile which Sara saw, a harsh implacable
profile etched in granite.

They arrived at the hospital a quarter of an hour too
soon, but immediately upon John's giving his name he
and Sara were ushered into a large, airy room with a
beautifully-tiled floor and bamboo furniture. A large
desk occupied one corner of the room, the light from one
of the three windows falling on to it.

'You'll be meeting Doctor Brewerton, one of the
Medical Officers,' John told her. 'This is his private
room.'

He came in a few moments later, a stocky man of about
fifty-five with greying hair and thick-horn-rimmed
spectacles. His skin was rugged and lined; his eyes, deep-
set and penetrating, were of the darkest blue Sara had
ever seen. His manner with her was brusque; he regarded
her almost with indifference when shaking hands, and it
was very clear that he would far rather she was not here
at all, so that he could chat with John.

'It's good to see you,' he was saying even before he released Sara's hand. 'How long is it since you were here? And what brings you to town now?'

'I'll explain why I'm here later,' he said, glancing swiftly at Sara. 'For the present—I did tell you on the phone this morning that I'd like someone to take a look at Miss Chesworth——'

'John,' broke in the doctor, 'what more can anyone else do than what you've done already?'

John paused, but only for a second or two.

'Miss Chesworth knows I'm not a practising doctor. I'd appreciate it, Stephen, if you'd have one of the doctors take a look at her. That arm's not healed yet, and the fever brought her down. She could do with a pick-me-up, and I didn't happen to have one.'

Dr Brewerton shrugged resignedly, and rang a bell. A dusky nurse appeared and he gave her instructions. Sara rose at once and was conducted out of the office, along a corridor and taken into a waiting-room where she was told that she would not have to wait many minutes.

She sat down, thinking of John and the admission he had just made, that he was not a practising doctor, which was tantamount to admitting that he had been struck off the register. She caught her underlip between her teeth, fighting against the obvious—that he had done something which, in the medical profession, was considered a crime. Had someone reported him for neglect? Or was it some woman who had been responsible for his being struck off? It was too painful to consider and she thrust it aside. Yet never could she imagine his committing an act of neglect towards a patient. He was a surgeon . . . he could have made an error of judgement when performing an operation. . . . Conjecture, she decided, would get her no-where. In any case, a young doctor appeared, and spoke

to her with an American accent. Her arm was un-
bandaged, examined, then dressed again by a nurse.
The doctor had obviously been given instructions by his
superior, because he knew he was to provide her with a
tonic.

Less than twenty minutes after leaving the room where
John was she had reached it again, and had just lifted her
hand to knock on the door when she heard Sri's name
mentioned.

'Something must be done, then,' the doctor was saying
in response to what John had said. 'She's intelligent
enough to be educated, so we'll have her brought down
here.'

'I'm troubled about the change. She's never been out
of the *ulu*, not even for a day. I ought to have brought her.
I think that perhaps I shall do just that, Stephen, bring
her here and stay with her for a while. Then she can be
left with some suitable family and sent to be educated.
It's essential that she is educated, because if she isn't the
marriage can't possibly survive.'

'No, I understand that, John.' There was a slight
pause and then, 'You've helped her a lot, but there are
limitations to what you can do. In any case, she needs
tutoring by an experienced teacher. Don't worry, I'll do
what I can. And I agree that you should bring her here
and stay with her for a while, since it'll all be so bewilder-
ing to her.'

'Thanks, Stephen. I'm grateful for your help.'

'This other girl—You said something on the phone
about her being a journalist. Why is she here—or rather,
why was she with the Ubani Ulu?'

'There was only one reason, Stephen. The British
Press——' John stopped abruptly and Sara, colouring
hotly at the idea of eavesdropping, knocked and entered

the room without giving the doctor any time to invite her in.

As soon as they had left the hospital John said grimly,

'How much did you overhear while I was with Stephen?'

She started, taken unawares.

'I—er—nothing. . . .' The stumbling negative faded out as she heard his furious intake of breath.

'I should have thought that past experience would have taught you that I've a sixth sense,' he rasped. 'I suddenly knew you'd come back and were outside that door!'

They were walking across the compound towards the place where their taxi waited. His stride was long and Sara was skipping to keep apace with him. She had gone hot, cursing herself for not realising—from past experience, as he had said—that he had that sixth sense. When she had taken that first shot with the camera he had known instantly and come crashing like an enraged jungle beast and snatched it from her. And the second time he would have known, but he was taking aim at the wild boar. Immediately afterwards, though, Sara had been warned by the quiver of a nerve spring that he sensed the presence of someone or something other than the animal he had killed, and she had prudently hidden the camera and stepped forth. So she should have foreseen that her presence outside that door would register with that sixth sense he mentioned. And yet here, in this atmosphere of civilisation, and dressed as he was, like any ordinary European, he seemed different, and she felt she was to be forgiven for losing sight of his jungle background and the keen alertness acquired because of it.

'I'm sorry,' was all she could find to say as she was ushered, none too gently, into the back seat of the taxi.

'I asked how much you'd heard!'

She hesitated, but sliding him a glance she decided not to make any further attempt to deceive a man with his uncanny instincts.

'You were talking about Sri,' she began, then told him all that she had overheard.

'You deliberately listened.' At the acid contempt in his voice she felt her colour rise. 'Have you no shame?'

'I'm sorry,' she muttered again. 'I haven't any other excuse than that I've been intrigued by your relationship with Sri from the very first.'

'Why? What business is it of yours?' Although a sort of grim hauteur edged his tone this time, Sara had the impression that he meant the question quite literally, that he was profoundly interested to know what business it was of hers.

It was almost as if he were pumping her about her feelings for him! And as she dwelt on this for a long moment she realised that she had gained the same impression once or twice before.

She said, watching his set, granite-like profile,

'It isn't any concern of mine. I agree with you that I ought to mind my own business.'

The taxi was wending its way along the street, and as John seemed disinclined to continue the conversation she leant back and looked through the window. They were travelling along the longest and most picturesque street in the capital, with shops selling local work and curios and pretty silver jewellery. Glimpses of old China depicted by Chinese temples could be seen. Sara had visited one or two of these temples while she was in Kuching, after their arrival, and had been pleasantly surprised by the attitude of the temple guardians, who seemed exceedingly happy to welcome visitors. In the

main bazaar there had been pandemonium, she recalled
wryly, with the haggling and bargaining of numerous
races and sub-races—Chinese, Malays, Hindus, Sikhs,
Dyaks, Javanese and many more, all neatly dressed,
jostling and gesticulating, creating a kaleidoscope of
colour and a cacophony of noise.

John had the taxi driver stop at the travel agents' and
they went in. There was no flight for two days. Sara
hesitated when John asked if she wanted to book a seat
on that particular plane and she found herself asking him
how long he was intending to stay in the capital.

He looked at her with an odd expression and she
added, awkwardly,

'If you were staying, I'd like to stay—that is, if you
wanted me—er—what I mean is——'

'What you're trying to ask, Sara, is whether or not I'd
like to have the pleasure of your company for a few days.'
He was regarding her in some amusement and he looked
so attractive that Sara's heart gave a little jerk, but her
response to his humour was a conventional smile which
gave nothing away—or she hoped it didn't!

'I wouldn't stay on my own,' she admitted, 'because
there isn't really much to do. But if I had company I'd
like to explore beyond the immediate capital. I'm sure
there's a lot to see.' Her thoughts went to Sri and with
some reluctance she added, 'I suppose I oughtn't to try
to persuade you, John, because of your wife.'

At that his grey eyes flickered strangely and he seemed
for a fleeting moment to be on the point of some disclosure, but a frown knit his brow and all he said was,

'If I were eager to get back to Sri nothing would prevent me from doing so. However, I feel like a break—I
do usually stay for about a week when I come to Kuching
or Sibu or any of the other towns.'

Sara looked at the assistant, who was waiting for her to make up her mind.

'You'll be staying, then?' she said, and John nodded at once.

'Get the plane that leaves a week today,' he advised. 'We'll have a break together.'

The business was conducted and they were back in the taxi when Sara said, turning to him,.

'You're obviously not angry then, about my—my listening?'

'I believe I understand,' was his cryptic reply, and although Sara would have liked to ask him what he meant she refrained. As far as he was concerned the matter was ended and quite naturally she was glad.

Nevertheless, she could not help recalling what she had overheard. It would seem that John was not at all happy with things as they were and he was intending that Sri should be educated. But would she ever come up to the sort of standard which a man like him would—or should —want? She had been born and bred a Native, a savage, and it could not be expected that education of any kind, begun now, when she was fifteen, could completely erase a background like that.

CHAPTER TEN

The next morning John announced that he had to see a friend, but Sara could come with him if she liked. Reluctant at first, she agreed only when she was convinced, by his encouraging smile, that he really desired her company. Her emotions were conflicting, for on the one hand something wonderful and exciting was welling up inside her, but on the other hand she felt deeply the futility of a happiness that could only be fleeting, because John was tied to another girl, a mere child, trusting and beautiful.

However, the time was now, she decided, and allowed herself the joy of his company, putting everything else from her mind except the fact that she had a full week to look forward to . . . a week of his companionship.

The friend he spoke of lived in a beautiful modern villa in a lovely coastal village of Cantobung, and John hired a car to get them there, driving it himself. They drove through pepper and sago plantations, areas of coconut palms and fruit trees.

'You've been along here before, when you first came to Kuching?' John asked.

'No, I didn't do much sightseeing at all, except in the city itself. I visited some of the temples.'

'You'll notice,' he remarked, 'that all the plantations have a rather attractive house attached.'

'Yes, and it's all very different from the jungle, isn't it?'

'Of course.'

'You like being here?' she ventured, and he turned briefly, to look at her in profile.

'What made you ask that, Sara?'

'I suppose,' she replied frankly, 'I was thinking that as long as you must live here, in Sarawak, you could just as easily have lived closer to civilisation.'

'But it was the jungle that drew me in the first place. I visited a friend in Brunei and we travelled into the *ulu*. The aspect, unsullied by so-called progress, the simple people who had their priorities right, the lack of pressure and of risks——' He stopped and the ensuing silence was not at all pleasant, nor were his thoughts, Sara decided, noticing the harsh set of his profile, the convulsive movements of his fingers round the wheel of the car. Plainly he was in the grip of some fierce and deep emotion. 'Yes, the certainty that the only risks one would encounter would be physical ones, and these could be dealt with——' he glanced at her, 'as your injuries were dealt with. But when risks affect the heart and the mind. . . .' He stopped again, this time slowly, the words fading into memory, and for one terrible moment there was sheer murder in his face, in the twist of the lips, the rigidity of the jaw, the brooding embers in his eyes as he flashed her a glance before concentrating on a dangerous bend.

No more was said. Sara sensed at once that he wanted to be quiet, to re-live something that had happened in the past.

The house was reached after a drive of about twenty miles. John turned into a drive lined by tall coconut palms and brought the car to a stop on a small square of pebble-covered ground at the front of the house.

Sara looked at it, thinking she would not be averse to living in Sarawak if she could have a beautiful home like this. It was a two-storied house, white with smooth pillars supporting a porch with a verandah above it. John's friend, an Englishman, was a veterinary officer working for the Sarawak Government on a livestock station; he was on vacation, John had said as they came along. His name was Eric Haynes; he was unmarried, had a Chinese housekeeper and a Dyak boy who looked after the garden.

Eric was younger than Sara had expected—about twenty-seven, she estimated. He greeted her with a ready smile, allowing his appreciative eyes to sweep over her from head to foot, in a matter of seconds.

'Welcome, Miss Chesworth. John phoned last evening to say he was bringing a newly-acquired friend.' He cast a curious glance in John's direction as he added, 'Feel yourself honoured, Miss Chesworth, as he isn't one for the ladies.'

She flashed John a glance, opened her mouth to remind Eric that he was married and then, for some inexplicable reason, she closed it again.

Eric ushered them on to a patio where they relaxed in the shade on garden loungers and drank iced orange juice. John had previously told Sara that Eric knew she was a journalist, but John had merely said she had been sent to Sarawak by her newspaper to get an article that would give a general picture of the country, an explanation which Eric appeared to accept with a sort of casual interest which was rather surprising to Sara.

'You ought to have come down for the Regatta,' Eric was saying conversationally to his friend. 'It was exceptionally good this year.'

'I should have done,' John admitted, 'but one becomes lethargic at times, living up there, away from reality.'

Eric laughed, and looked at Sara.

'How did you like the far interior? Did you get all you wanted?' And before she had time to answer he was saying, 'It's amazing what women will tackle these days. Proves they were always capable, doesn't it?'

'Yes, we were always capable,' she agreed, and just had to add, 'But men wouldn't until recently accept that we were.'

'And it isn't accepted everywhere even now, not by any means.' Eric smiled faintly and cast a glance at his friend. 'Where you are, for example, the women are kept under.'

John shrugged his shoulders and changed the subject, plainly not wanting to talk about women. He asked Eric about his job and for the next five minutes or so Sara sat back in her chair, listening to the conversation and at the same time casting her eyes around in appreciation of the lovely gardens which were a glory of tropical flowers and trees. Sun-birds and flycatchers flitted about, their colours iridescent in the brittle rays of the sun. Beautiful butterflies hovered over the flowers, and in the trees the incessant drilling of cicadas contributed to the unreality of the atmosphere. How different from London! From her flat in a tall Victorian house whose view was on to other houses, with in the distance huge piles of concrete fashioned to accommodate hundreds upon hundreds of office workers. Here, all was peace, with no overcrowding, no rat-race, no one vying with another in the race for social or material superiority. Nature was supreme, its gifts and treasures incomparable. True, it had its less attractive side, when black storms attacked the land, lashing it with hurricanes of wind, illuminating it with fitful streaks of lightning or blasting it with shattering roars of thunder. The drenching rain filled the rivers, often to overflowing, but in spite of all this the compensations were innumerable.

'You've solved the problem completely, then?' John's quiet voice drifted unbidden into Sara's reverie and she found her interest transferred to what the men were discussing.

'Yes; it's taken a long time, but the fight against the disease is over at last.'

'So we can see a great increase in our livestock population in the not-so-distant future?'

'In cattle production, certainly.'

'You must feel gratified at your success.'

Sara, listening more intently than she had supposed, caught the note of discord in John's tone. Was he envying his friend the valuable work he was doing in delving into animal diseases and finding cures against their ravages? All the small farmers must be grateful to him and his colleagues. He was doing good all the time, living a useful existence.

'I do indeed. It was a triumph when we could say for sure that the disease was overcome.'

They chatted on. Eric wanted them to stay for lunch, but although Sara would have liked to accept the invitation John declined it, giving as an excuse that he had business to do in Kuching.

'The next time, then, John.' Eric saw them to the car, telling John to come more often, as all his friends would like to see him. 'You shut yourself off too much,' he added finally. 'Don't do it.'

That evening Sara and John dined at a Chinese restaurant in the town, then strolled back to the hotel.

'Do you want to go in, Sara?'

It was early and the sky was lit with a million stars. Sara, desiring nothing more than to be with him, in the hotel gardens, was at the same time profoundly conscious that he had a wife. In addition she knew she must guard against a deepening of her feelings for him. This week was madness and she had known it from the first. But she could not have resisted having it with John no matter how hard she had tried. It was so much easier to agree to stay than to make the decision to leave. She would have to leave, of course, and had already sent the cable to Joe to say she was returning, but had refrained from saying anything about her failure. It was a case of first things first; she wanted the memories which this inter-

lude with John would bring to her. As for his feelings
for her—she would have been blind indeed if she had
not noticed the unguarded glances, the inflections in his
voice, the faint sighs which could have meant regret, and
resignation. He would never hurt his wife; of that Sara
was absolutely certain, so there was no hope, no, not
even if he *were* falling in love with her.

'I asked you a question,' he murmured. They were
walking towards the lights of the hotel, but he slowed the
pace right down and she had to do the same. And then
he stopped altogether.

'I—I. . . .' She turned to him in the shadows of a
jacaranda tree, its lovely fern-like foliage forming a star-
spangled ceiling above the handsome grey-barked trunk
and branches. 'John, it's—I mean, there's nothing for—
for us to—to stay out here for——' Her words were cut as
he took her hand, bringing her unresistingly towards
him.

'We can walk, and talk,' he said quietly, tilting her
chin with his hand, looking into her eyes before bending
his head and touching her lips with his. Vibrations rippled
through her; Sri was forgotten in the urgent desire of the
moment as she clung to him, offering her lips, inviting
with her eyes.

He kissed her passionately and for a long time they
stood very close, John kissing, caressing, tempting her to
a point where surrender was just a dream away. Nothing
mattered except this moment. People, places, obligations
. . . all were alienated from the bliss and ecstasy that
could be hers if she decided to succumb to the primitive
desires that were gripping her. But she found herself
saying bleakly, allowing her mind to drift from the
enchantment of the present to the inevitable bitterness
and regret of the future,

'I want to go in, John. Shall we sit in the lounge and have a drink——'

'You knew, Sara,' he broke in softly, 'that if we had this holiday together the outcome would be——'

'No, no, I didn't!' she broke in before he could finish, 'I only wanted your company, not—not—your—your lovemaking.'

'You little liar,' he said softly, his lips caressing her hot cheek. 'Up there, you'd have given yourself to me and you know it. You were saved by the storm—if saved is the right word, which I very much doubt. More likely you were as disappointed as I was.'

'Don't you ever think of your wife?' she flashed, his cool confidence provoking her to anger.

'Often,' he returned bitterly, and Sara gave a start. For there was some underlying emotion in his voice which convinced her that it was not Sri he was referring to at all. And then he added, 'But what the eye doesn't see the heart doesn't grieve over.' And this time it was Sri, it must be, because he was endeavouring to persuade her, Sara, to forget her scruples and have an affair with him.

'How can you talk like that?' The magic was gone, obliterated by words she hated to hear from the man she had come to respect. He had been so gentle with Sri, so very kind. But he did not love her, nor was he content with her any more, so he was intending that she should be educated. A sigh escaped Sara, for none of it made much sense at all. She said, speaking her thoughts aloud but not meaning to,

'I suppose you've gone so far back to the primitive state that you don't expect much any more?'

'Eh?' He looked questioningly at her, holding her away from him but not releasing her even though she tried to pull right away. 'What are you talking about?'

'Sri—you want her educated. You know I overheard it all—when you were discussing it. I suppose when Sri was crying it had something to do with it——' She spread her hands in a gesture of frustration. 'I don't understand you—or anything about you!'

'That's only to be expected,' he returned in a brooding tone she failed utterly to interpret. 'However, let's put an end to this and go inside, as you suggest. It's safer for us both.'

The next morning Sara awoke to a feeling of deep depression which even the liquid song of the yellow-crowned bulbul did nothing to dispel. She knew she had made a mistake in wanting to stay for this week, and it struck her that there might be time to book a seat on the plane that was scheduled for tomorrow. She would mention it at breakfast, she decided, and see how John reacted. She rather thought he would be relieved if she could get the plane, since the situation seemed to have changed between them, changed because of last night. Had he really believed that her reason for wanting this week with him was that they would indulge in an affair? She wondered how she would have fared if they had been up there, in his hut, where he could have taken her by force if he wanted to.

He was already in the restaurant when she entered; he rose at once and she sat down, bidding him good morning. After returning the greeting he subjected her to a long and searching scrutiny and said,

'So you've decided to try for the plane that leaves tomorrow?'

She gave a start.

'You're uncanny,' she complained, ruffled by his perception.

'That sixth sense I spoke about.' He picked up the menu, but instead of reading it he continued to regard Sara from over the top of it. 'I suppose it would be best if you left tomorrow. And yet I shall miss you, Sara——' He stopped and a mirthless laugh escaped him. 'I thought at one time that I would be wise to kill you. I'm glad I didn't.' So casual! Did he mean it?

'Are you serious?' she asked, examining his sun-bitten face, his long hair, his sharply-defined features, carved like granite. The mark of the heathen was there, plain in every respect but most of all in those grey eyes that were deep and unfathomable . . . and often smouldering. 'Would you have killed me, in cold blood?'

'What do you think?' he challenged.

She licked her lips, shivering inwardly at the expression on his face.

'I believe you would,' she murmured after a pause. 'Yes, John . . . I think you would. . . .'

'As I said, I'm glad I didn't.' He was suppressing laughter all at once and, staggered by the change, she realised that he had been playing with her, deriving enjoyment by convincing her that he could commit murder.

'You wouldn't have killed me!' she snapped, taking up her menu and turning the cover wrathfully.

'Your common sense ought to have told you that,' he remarked with a hint of derision. 'We do happen to have some degree of law and order up in the *ulu*. I did tell you that we're under the jurisdiction of the authorities in Kuching.'

'You also said that the laws aren't very effective, because you live so far into the interior,' she reminded him.

'Do you really suppose I'd risk imprisonment?'

She shook her head impatiently.

'No, I suppose not,' shortly and with an indication that the subject ought to be dropped. 'About my going home tomorrow——'

'I don't know if you'll be able to get on the plane, but if you want to try we can instruct the hotel people to get through to the airport for you.'

She looked at him, his sudden indifference a knife in her heart. She did not often feel sorry for herself, but she feared she would find relief in tears when once she found herself alone.

But as it happened she had no opportunity of indulging herself in that way, for no sooner had she come from the restaurant than she was told by a porter that she was wanted at the desk.

'A cable for you, Miss Chesworth.' It was handed to her. John was right behind her, but he moved away.

She said a moment later, turning to him,

'I can't go tomorrow. One of our reporters is on his way here. Joe has decided to send him. He must have become worried about me. Yet I did say that I wouldn't be in touch. You see, I didn't know where I'd be——'

'You said you'd sent a cable to your editor,' interrupted John shortly. 'If he's received it then why should he be worried?'

'Graham was already on his way here when Joe received it and there was no way of recalling him. As you know, the flight takes over twenty-four hours.' She stopped, deep anxiety shading her eyes. 'Graham Findlay's the last one Joe ought to have sent; he knows very well I don't like him. He's one of those reporters, John, who's totally unscrupulous, who'll go to any lengths to get a story.' She went on to explain her dislike, saying that Graham had no conscience and if he could steal another's story he would not hesitate to do so. 'No one likes him—except Joe, and that's only because he manages to get such good scoops.'

John was looking thoughtful.

'You think that once he learns that you didn't get a story he'll set about trying to get one himself?'

She nodded.

'Definitely. He won't hestitate.'

John moved away from the desk and she followed him to a table in the lounge where they sat down. John was still thoughtful, his eyes narrowed, his lips pursed.

'On the surface,' he commented at length, 'it would seem that the sole purpose for his coming here is to make sure that you're safe?'

'Yes, that would be one of Joe's reasons for sending him——'

'One?'

'Joe would know that, if it so happened that I had failed to get a story, Graham would be more successful.'

'Such is his reputation, eh?'

She nodded, anger bringing colour to her face.

'Joe knows I dislike Graham intensely!'

'But a newspaper editor has to get stories, Sara.'

She looked at him.

'You're so calm about it,' she said, almost accusingly.

'Why not? When you think about it in a little more depth, as I've been doing these past few minutes, you discover that there isn't a thing to worry about.'

She shook her head in bewilderment.

'He'll go all out to get your story!' she flashed, putting force into her words in order to make him aware of the danger.

'And where,' enquired John casually, 'is he going to make a start?'

'Well . . . here, I suppose.'

'But the white man he's interested in lives up in the interior of the jungle.'

Sara looked at his hair, at the glossy bronzed skin, sun-bitten and tough.

'John,' she said seriously, 'you have no idea of that man's uncanny reasoning power, his intuition. He hasn't earned his reputation for nothing. He'll be staying here, in this hotel, naturally, because I'm here. When he sees you—and especially if I'm with you—he'll know immediately that you're the white man who's living with the Natives.'

'Nonsense!' he said derisively almost before she had finished speaking. 'You're letting your anxiety get the better of your common sense! There are about sixty or seventy people staying in this hotel, so how the devil is he going to pick me out and say this is the man who's living in the jungle—No, don't interrupt me, Sara! I don't give a damn for this uncanny insight, or whatever you call it! He'd have to be omniscient to know who I am.'

She was still troubled; it showed in her shadowed eyes, in the faint movement of her mouth.

'I feel, John, that you should leave here and go back to the *ulu*. I don't know if Joe's given him permission to go up into the jungle—if Graham finds I haven't got the story—but, up there, you'll be better able to deal with him.'

'I haven't the slightest intention of going back until I'm ready. Most certainly I shan't be driven back by any damned reporter!' He looked at her and the anger left his face. 'I'm having this week with you, Sara, and no Press man from the *Sunday Sphere*'s going to interfere with either of us. And,' he added as an afterthought, 'he can find his own entertainment while you're waiting for your flight. He mustn't expect you to entertain him.'

'He'll keep himself entertained,' she persisted. 'He'll make all sorts of enquiries, no matter what you say. He'll ask all about, go into the back streets and question all sorts of people—Oh, John, I wish you'd take notice of me!' she cried in desperation. 'I know him and you don't!'

'Nor do I want to,' was John's calm rejoinder. 'He sounds just about the worst of his type.'

'I shall have it out with Joe when I get back,' she said determinedly. 'He could have sent someone else, if he was so worried about me! There were several of my male colleagues who badly wanted the assignment, but Joe chose me——'

'He chose you—from among several men?' He looked at her curiously. 'Men wanted the job and yet he gave it to a woman?'

'We do have equality,' Sara reminded him with a hint of tartness in her voice.

Ignoring that, he said softly,

'Was there any particular reason for his giving you the assignment?'

'No—er. ... .' The colour was rising in her cheeks. The idea of lying was dismissed, although it would have been far easier than saying, 'Well, yes, there was a reason. What I mean is—he was beginning to—er—to like me.'

'He fell in love with you?' sharply and with an un-expected hint of suppressed violence in his tone.

She nodded, averting her head against the uncomfort-able, searching expression in his eyes.

'Yes—I think it was only infatuation, really,' she answered with haste. 'He's happily married and has two lovely children.'

'Why did he have to resort to such drastic measures as

to send you off to the other side of the world?' he demanded grimly. 'Were his feelings reciprocated?'

'No, certainly not!'

'You sound very vehement about it.' There was a distinct glimmer in his eye and an imperious under-current in his manner. 'Are you sure you weren't in love with him? You certainly appear to be on more than ordinarily close terms with him.'

'Close!' she flashed. 'No such thing!'

'Yet you decided to accept the assignment and come away for a while.'

Sara drew a breath.

'You're too astute,' she complained. 'All right, then! I did come because of the situation! But there'd never have been an affair, if that's what you think!' She stopped, censure in her eyes, and when she resumed, her voice was far from steady. 'It isn't very nice of you to—to suggest that I'm like that—Oh, I don't want to talk about it—if you don't mind!'

'All right! There's no need for all these dramatics.' She said nothing and he added quietly, 'You said I was astute, but there isn't anything unusually astute in my deduction, Sara. I've often wondered what prompted you to take on a job with the obvious risks this one entailed. I see now that you considered it prudent to get away. But now,' he said, a grimness creeping into his voice, 'you're going back. What's going to happen?' His regard was keen and questioning, with flecks of steel glinting in his eyes. He was angry . . . and he was jealous. . . .

She said quiveringly,

'I'm hoping that Joe will have got over it.'

'You haven't been away long enough for him to have got over it,' he stated in a tone that warned her not to argue the point.

'Well, there's nothing I can do about it,' she pointed out, repressing a sigh of impatience.

John studied her, noticing the flush on her cheeks, the way her underlip was caught between her teeth.

'You're not troubled about finding yourself in the sort of situation which existed before?'

'It might not be the same——'

'It will!' imperiously and again in a tone that warned her not to argue.

'You seem so sure!' she flashed pettishly. 'And there's no valid reason why you should be!'

'No . . .?' A small silence ensued, with John seeming to become totally detached from everything in the vicinity. 'I can't conceive,' he murmured at last, and speaking to himself, 'that anyone who fell in love with you could get over it in a hurry. . . .'

Sara's heart gave a little jerk.

'What—what are you s-saying—John——?' She shook her head instantly, for engraved on her mind was the image of Sri. 'It doesn't matter! Don't answer me! We were talking about Graham, and I was telling you that he'd try——'

'I thought,' broke in John, lifting a lean brown hand to suppress a yawn, 'that we'd finished talking about Graham.'

'But——'

'The subject bores me,' he protested, having first silenced her by an imperious flick of his fingers. 'It was something different altogether that we were talking about.'

Sara threw him a direct look.

'You have a lovely wife,' she reminded him gently, at which a frown touched his brow, only to be gone instantly.

'We don't seem to be getting very far,' he said. 'I'd planned to enjoy ourselves today. I want to take you to one of the beaches.'

She gave a small sigh. It seemed futile to attempt any more to persuade him that he ought to guard against the scheming of Graham Findlay, but she did try once more, bringing to his notice the fact that his name was in the hotel register. He gave a small start and at first she knew a sense of satisfaction that she had at last succeeded in awakening him to the possible danger. However, when he spoke it was to say, in a quiet, unhurried tone of voice,

'Parker's the name I'm known as here. Only my bank manager is in possession of my real name.'

She stared, recalling that she had decided that, if she wished, she could find out all about him once she was back in England—could discover just who John Parker was.

'It's not your real name?' Something else she was remembering was the way he had avoided her eyes when telling her his name.

'Obviously if a man wishes to lose himself the first thing he must do is assume another name.' That was all. He changed the subject, telling her a little about the places and sights they would be passing as he drove her in the car he had hired, to the beach. He also told her that she would have to be satisfied with sunbathing, as he would not allow her to get the bandage wet. She felt she could manage to float without getting it wet, but when she argued he assured her quietly that she would do as she was told.

'A patient never argues with her doctor,' he added finally. They were in the car by this time, leaving the lovely gardens of the hotel to drive along the main street before taking the road which ran parallel to the coast.

She coloured at his authoritative words. His manner verged on the intimate, this attitude of mastery and imperiousness he was adopting with her. He glanced sideways at her, a warning in his eye, as if he were expecting some further argument and he was telling her beforehand not to waste her time on anything so fruitless.

'I've brought my swimsuit,' she ventured to say. 'It's in the beach bag.'

'If I'd known you were intending bringing it I'd have told you not to bother.'

She drew a breath, and moved the beach bag with her foot in a gesture of annoyance that brought a laugh from her companion.

But he made no comment and soon afterwards he was parking the car beneath some trees. They walked the short distance to the beach where John discarded slacks and shirt, dropping them on to a towel which he had put on the sand. Sara looked at him, catching her breath at the perfection of his teak-brown body, gleaming in the sun. It could have belonged to one of the Natives, she thought, responding to the smile he flashed her, a smile that revealed perfect, strong white teeth.

'Sit there and relax,' he advised. 'You worry too much, child. You ought to know me well enough by now to be convinced that I could deal with a dozen Grahams if need be!' He laughed and again her breath caught at the attractiveness of him. And then a wave of sheer misery flooded her whole mind and body. To have fallen in love with him, and now to part, never to see him again. She was crucified by her own thoughts as she visualised the lonely years ahead—she in England and he thousands of miles away in the jungle of Borneo . . . with his lovely young wife. . . . There would be children, eventually, when Sri was older, children who would probably be sent to Kuching to be educated, but who would be Natives for all that.

She cast it all from her and watched John instead as he swam strongly away from the shore. Was any man so perfect! She wondered if it was the life in the jungle which had given him such a fine body. He was active up there, swimming, hunting, taking his *prahu* along the treacherous rivers. Yes, a life like that, lived mainly out of doors, was bound to give a man a healthy, sun-bronzed body.

He was coming back to her; she felt an absurd rush of tears and it was with the greatest difficulty that she managed to keep her depression from him. She watched him spring on to the shore from a rock, then stride with a sort of negligent ease to where he had left his towel. He took it up, letting his clothes fall on to the sand. Sara watched as he rubbed himself down, saw him take the long dark hair and dry it briskly between the folds of the towel.

'You look so like a Native,' she could not help saying.

'Many Natives,' he reminded her, 'are very civilised.'

'I wasn't implying that you were not.'

'I wish you were staying longer. I'd take you around the other districts. You're going back having seen nothing of our country.' She made no comment and he went on, 'In many districts live Dyaks who were once famous as headhunters and pirates, but now they're respected, well-to-do men, Christians and highly educated.' He told her that some longhouses had their own power stations, and that Dyaks owned all the shops in the district.

Sara still said nothing and eventually he was saying that he supposed she was thinking he needed a haircut.

'I don't know. It suits you—at least, when you're in the jungle.'

'But not here, in the world of civilisation?'

'Your friends don't seem to notice.'

'If they do they're too polite to comment.' He continued rubbing, then took a comb from a pocket in his trunks and drew it through his hair. 'You look adorable,' he murmured, staring down at her, his eyes wandering with unveiled admiration. She was sitting on a towel, clad in a short sun-dress, her knees drawn up to her chin, her arms hugging them. The sun was on her hair, accentuating its glorious colour. Her skin was honey-bronze, clear and delicate. And she was managing to smile, and if it were tears that caused the brightness in her eyes John was ignorant of it. All he saw was a beautiful picture, and he told her so. She coloured and lowered her head. He bent and tilted her chin, then swung his body round and down so that he was sitting beside her, her chin still in his hand. 'How old are you, Sara?' he asked, his eyes holding hers in a steady, compelling gaze.

'Twenty-five.'

'Twenty-five,' he repeated slowly and thoughtfully. He seemed to swallow a lump in his throat and the silence stretched. He released her chin; she could still feel the warmth, and slight dampness of his fingers. She said, forced to break the silence,

'You, John—how old are you?'

He hesitated, but only for a moment.

'Thirty-seven.'

She nodded reflectively.

'I took a guess that you were over thirty and under forty,' she said.

'It's a long time since I was thirty.' Bitterness touched his voice; she estimated that he would be about thirty when it happened . . . whatever it was that happened.

'You have no regrets about coming here—into the jungle, I mean?'

'Under the circumstances, no.'

The moment was intimate. She knew there would be no danger of a snub if she asked him why he came. And yet the words could not be spoken, because she did not want to hear that he had done something so very discreditable that he had been struck off the medical register.

But she did say, hesitantly, and a little apprehensively,

'Were you ever married before, John—when you were in England, I mean?'

He nodded, his eyes brittle hard.

'Yes, Sara, I was.' He turned from her to stare out to sea. 'It seems a long time ago. . . . So long. . . .' He was on his own, remote from her, and she dared not try to bring him back. 'How little we guess what our fate will be! Yet if we knew beforehand what could we do to alter it? Nothing, because we're merely pawns in the hands of destiny.'

A long silence ensued before he turned to her, a reluctant smile breaking, erasing the tautness that had made his profile appear so harsh. 'Yes, Sara, I was married once, and happy. I seemed to have just about everything a man could have, but it proved to be a fool's paradise I was living in, a cosy little world which bred complacency. I thought nothing could go wrong.'

He got up and pulled her up beside him. There were a few other people on the beach, but they were a good distance away. He stood close, gazing down into her face.

She quivered at his touch, at the nearness of his body, and she closed her eyes tightly, to prevent the ready tears from falling.

'Why didn't I meet you then——?' He stopped abruptly, bent down to pick up the towel, and said brusquely, 'Come on, Sara. It's time we were thinking about some lunch!'

CHAPTER ELEVEN

THEY had lunch together, then John said he had some business to do and he would be with her later.

'Can you amuse yourself for a couple of hours?' he asked, smiling at her as they sat in the lounge, having just finished their coffee.

'Yes, of course. . . .' Sara paused a moment. 'John. . . .'

'Yes?'

'Graham—you haven't made any plans.'

'Yes, I have. I shall tell you about them when I see you in a couple of hours' time.' He had earlier made enquiries about the time of arrival of the reporter's plane and had been told it would arrive at a quarter past six that evening, if it was on time.

'You've something in mind, then?'

'My dear Sara,' he returned with some asperity, 'don't fuss!' He glanced at his watch. 'I must go. I have to see someone and it's important. Sorry to be leaving you, but it isn't for long.'

She wandered about the town on her own, looking at the temples, standing before one in particular, the

Temple of Hian Tien Shian Tee—God of Heaven—which she had been into during that week she was in Kuching before she had gone up into the jungle. She was recalling what the smiling guardian of the temple had told her about the various celebrations that were held there. Every year on the third day of the third moon the birthday of Shian Tee was celebrated, and his death on the ninth day of the ninth moon. There were others, all according to the Chinese calendar, which was ruled by the moons.

She moved on after a while, allowing her thoughts to wander where they would, with the result that they flitted about, and first they were on this business which had taken John away; she was sure it had something to do with Sri, but the reason for her conviction eluded her. She was next thinking of Graham and wishing with all her heart he was not coming. That John was so complacent about it troubled her, knowing Graham as she did. He had a 'nose' for a story, and a great deal of luck—which in the opinion of his colleagues he did not need! Sara put his image from her mind in favour of a dark satanic face . . . the face of a heathen. . . . She heard again his words,

'Why didn't I meet you then——?'

No mistaking the meaning, nor the look he gave her at the time the words were spoken. A shuddering sigh escaped from the very depths of her. Everything was wrong, and she felt it would be wrong for a long while to come. She could never forget John, and this meant that no other man would ever mean anything to her.

She reached the hotel a few minutes before him, and gave an involuntary gasp of disbelief when she saw him walk casually into the lounge where she was waiting.

'Your hair!' she exclaimed, staring up from the depths

of her armchair. 'You look so different!'

'An improvement, I hope.'

She nodded, but doubtfully.

'It suits you here, and those clothes, but in the jungle—well, the long hair is—er——' She stopped, not quite knowing what she wanted to say.

'Is more fashionable,' he finished for her, laughing in a way that set her heartbeats racing.

'The men won't know you.'

'I do happen to have had haircuts before,' he said. 'It would have been down to my ankles if I hadn't.'

He called for afternoon tea and while they waited for it he began to speak, telling her that at one time he had been on the resident staff of archaeologists who were excavating in the Niah Caves. Sara had read about the excavations, her imagination stimulated by the fact that so much evidence had been unearthed of human activity as long ago as 50,000 B.C.

'I envy you,' she said, aware that she was not altogether surprised to learn that he had been engaged on useful work for the Sarawak Government.

'It's interesting. I still go back periodically and have a few weeks there. However, I merely mentioned the caves in passing. What I want to say is that I've rung my friend who's in charge of the diggings and told him that, should anyone enquire about me, I'm employed on the excavations but am at present on vacation, taking a holiday in Kuching. It's merely a precaution, and it gives you something to tell this colleague of yours to explain my presence here, because he'll obviously ask you who I am and how you come to be with me. You'll say that we met casually, here in the hotel, and as I was alone and you were waiting for a flight back to England, we got together and are going about—I did tell you you weren't giving him any of your time,' he reminded her imperiously.

'Yes, John, you did.' She had listened to him, wide-eyed, unable to find a flaw in his plan and wondering why she had doubted his ability to thwart Graham—should he become suspicious.

'You approve of my plan?' he said, and she nodded instantly.

'It's marvellous! You're safe from his prying.'

'I'd have been safe anyway,' he assured her grimly. 'It would take more than this fellow to get the better of me!'

'And we can have our holiday together. Oh, John, I'm so glad! And relieved! I was dreadfully troubled about you, feeling it was all my fault for coming in the first place.'

'Don't blame yourself, dear,' he said gently. 'I'm glad you came, as it's turned out. We've had pleasant times together——' He stopped, a thread of amusement creeping into the gravity of his voice. 'And some rather nasty little fights.'

She laughed, but shakily.

'You terrified me, John.'

'I could have killed you!'

'And hung my head in your hut.'

He frowned then, darkly.

'Let's forget the fights and remember only the pleasant times, shall we?' His eyes were grave again and so was his voice. 'I shall have some wonderful memories before we part, Sara, and I know you will have as well.'

She was too full to speak for a moment, and when eventually she did so it was to change the subject, since this one was too painful by far, bringing an ache to her heart and tears to her eyes.

'Graham's going to ask me if you know I'm a journalist. What shall I tell him, John?'

'I've been considering,' he admitted, 'and I feel that you ought to be casual about it, saying—if he does bring the question up—that although you've told me you're a journalist, you haven't said much else. Give him to understand that we're merely acquaintances, and therefore you haven't considered it necessary to confide in me anything about the nature of your present work.'

'He might think you can easily find out.'

'No.' John shook his head. 'Niah's a great distance from here and living there, close to the caves, I wouldn't know what was going on so far away.'

'I don't suppose,' said Sara, reflecting on Graham's tenacity when he was absorbed in a job, 'that he'll bother about such trivialities. He'll be too busy with other things.'

John passed that off. It was plain that he cared nothing for any activities which might occupy her colleague's time.

The tea came, and after a few moments of companionable silence Sara ventured to say,

'I felt, somehow, that you'd gone to do something for Sri.'

'You did?' he said in surprise. 'Well, as a matter of fact, I did do something for her.' That was all. He seemed pleased, but it was plain that he had no intention of talking about it to Sara. She looked at him, smart and immaculate in European clothes, his hair the conventional length, shining and well brushed, with the iron-grey at his temples, adding—if that were possible— to his air of distinction. An impressive man, one who would attract attention anywhere. He noticed her concentrated gaze and asked,

'What is it, dear?'

Dear. . . . It was the second time he had spoken the word in a matter of minutes.

She said, a smile on her lips but an ache in her heart, 'I'm happy at the idea of our being together for a little while, John.'

'So am I.' He looked at her face, his own becoming taut. A sigh escaped him, just as it had on other occasions, and this time Sara was in no doubt at all that it betrayed deep regret . . . for what might have been. 'Your dress is pretty,' he remarked, as if he had to say something.

'Thank you,' she smiled.

'You've got a beautiful tan; the white background of the dress brings it out most attractively.' His eyes settled on the bandaged arm. 'I hope your scars aren't too bad,' he said mechanically.

'I'm alive, and that's all I care about.'

The trace of a smile touched his lips.

'My experience of women,' he said in some amusement, 'is that while at first—after being disfigured—they're satisfied that they're alive, they very soon want to do something about the disfigurements once the novelty of being alive wears off.' He was laughing now, and Sara's breath caught at the attractiveness of the little crinkly lines fanning out from his eyes, at the absence of all harshness from his face.

'You've done plastic surgery?' she queried.

'You've guessed my line of business.'

'Restoring good looks is only secondary, I think,' she said, and John nodded at once.

'There are other, more important operations to perform. . . .' His voice trailed and he frowned. Gone was the amusement, he was staring into space, his thoughts not very pleasant at all, decided Sara perceptively. Had he made a mistake when performing an operation? She thrust the idea aside and said softly,

'I wish I'd known you in those days, John.'

He looked at her, the moment charged with tension. He opened his mouth to speak and she held her breath, waiting. But whatever words hovered on his tongue were never spoken. Other words, brusque and cold, came slowly, quietly and tinged with bitterness.

'We're mere pawns in the hands of destiny, as I've already said.' Picking up his cup he drank the contents, then replaced it on the saucer. 'Let's take a stroll through the town,' he suggested, making ready to rise as he saw that she had finished her tea. 'First, though, I must make a couple of phone calls. I want supplies from the hospital, for one thing, and supplies from the stores for another.' He paused to smile at her. 'Give me half an hour; I'll be in the lobby waiting for you at about a quarter past four.'

CHAPTER TWELVE

JOHN left her outside her room, but no sooner had she entered it than she remembered her handbag, which she must have left on the chair in the lounge. Hurriedly she got into the lift and pressed the button. To her relief her bag was there. She picked it up and was just about to cross the lobby to the lift when a taxi stopped at the front and she was hailed by Graham.

Here . . . already. . . . Her throat grew dry as she stood there, watching him enter, the porter carrying two large suitcases handed to him by the driver.

She braced herself for his greeting, and his questions. How she disliked him! His face was too big, his laugh too loud. And those deep-set ice-blue eyes that never gave anything away. He was thinning on top, although she doubted if he was much more than thirty.

'Sara! Hello! What are you doing here? I thought you'd be up in the jungle——' He stopped, frowning at her arm. 'What happened?'

She said it was nothing, having no patience to go into details while they were standing here, with people moving about around them, their interest caught owing to Graham's loudness of speech.

'I sent a cable to Joe telling him I was in Kuching.' She glanced around. 'We can't stand here.'

'No, of course not! Let me check in and get my room number and then we'll chat over drinks. Joe's given me all sorts of instructions, but I'll see what you have to say before I tell you about them!' He was all exuberance, as usual, she thought, wishing she had not forgotten her bag and had to come down for it. She went back into the lounge, where he joined her in less than five minutes.

'What are you having?' he wanted to know, beckoning to a passing waiter.

'Nothing, thanks; I've just had afternoon tea.'

'I'll have a whisky. Oh, but it's a bit of luck that you're here! However, tell me everything! I'm darned lucky to be sent out here. I wanted the job, as you know——' He stopped as the waiter came, and gave his order. 'Why are you here and not in the jungle?' he asked again. 'You must have got the story?' Nothing in his tone to denote disappointment, but Sara knew he was waiting, on tenterhooks, for her reply. Briefly she explained everything—the journey and its problems, with the Natives like clams whenever the white man was mentioned. She told him of the attack by the bear, and of the fever, skipping lightly over both and saying when he asked who had looked after her,

'The medicine-man,' and she felt sure John would congratulate her on that particular bit of subtlety.

'So you didn't do much at all about getting a story?' Graham took coins from his pocket as the waiter put his drink in front of him.

'I was fed up with the whole business. This——' she pointed to the bandage. 'I was clawed all over, but this was the worst. Then the fever, caused by shock, I suppose. I decided to call the whole thing off.'

'You never even met this bloke, then?' and without giving her time to answer he went on to say that Joe had had a hunch that she would fail, because he had had information that several other journalists had failed.

'He was worried about you,' he went on, 'but also he did want a story. So he sent me——'

'You asked him if you could come?'

'Clever girl!' He gave a crack of laughter which drew the attention of the four people sitting at an adjacent table. 'I was just itching to be on the scent!'

'I don't doubt it,' she returned drily.

'Don't be like that—bitchy—it's not you, Sara.'

She gave a small sigh, deciding to make an attempt to bring this conversation to a speedy end.

'What are Joe's instructions?' she asked, watching him pour a small amount of water into his glass.

'If you've failed I'm to have a free hand. He's given me a month.'

'Not long enough,' she declared. 'It'll take you a few days to organise the trip into the *ulu*—you'll need guides and the students are all back at college after the vacation. Then it's three days—or it could take four depending on the state of the rivers—to get into Ubani Ulu territory. And when you do you'll meet with hostility.' She was making it sound too difficult, and at the same time stressing the fact that it would prove to be an abortive venture anyway. But noticing his reaction—the pursing of his mouth, the vacancy of those cold blue eyes—she wondered why she had taken the trouble. Graham would do exactly what *he* wanted to do, regardless of any advice given, especially by her, whom he had never got on with, and never would. There was of course a veneer of cordiality covering both their approaches to one another; there had to be, seeing that they worked for the same newspaper and in the same office, but deep down there was not the smallest degree of love lost.

'I shall get a story,' he told her confidently. 'It wasn't a woman's task and I told Joe at the time. There are too many risks.' His eyes settled on the bandage for a space. 'Was it very bad?' he asked. She looked at him, realised that he was miles away, planning the trip into the jungle, and she knew that whatever answer she gave would hardly register, so she merely said,

'I've got over it, Graham.'

He talked on, about his plans, but then he startled her a little by saying he believed he would begin right here, in Kuching, startled her even though she had known he would begin here.

'This bloke'll be known by someone, surely. If as you say it's going to take several days to organise the trip into the jungle I might as well utilise my time profitably —if I can, that is. You're not leaving here for another six days, you say?'

'That's right.' She glanced at her watch. There was still fifteen minutes to go before she met John in the lobby.

'Then you can help me,' he said decisively. 'You can

go round to some of the shops and ask——'

'Nothing doing, Graham,' she interposed quietly. 'I'm not your stooge.'

'That's nice! What are you going to do with yourself if you don't give me assistance? Stick around doing nothing?'

'I'm having a holiday. I've earned it.'

'Joe won't be happy about that!'

'I've got myself a boy-friend,' she admitted casually. 'And he's showing me the sights.'

'A——?' He stared disbelievingly. 'Here? How come?'

'He's an archaeologist on vacation. We met here, in the hotel and—well—got together, sort of.'

'An archaeologist? Where from?'

'He's working on the excavations at the Niah Caves. They're a long way from here.'

'The Niah Painted Caves. . . . Yes,' he murmured, his thoughts far away, 'I know where they are. A lot's been written about them recently, in many parts of the world. They've become famous since they were discovered in 1958. Got their name from the fantastic murals—done in red haematite—on the limestone walls and ceilings of the caves. The archaeologists have unearthed amazing evidence of early human occupancy—over two hundred thousand pieces of pottery came to light early in the digging, if my memory serves me correctly.'

Which it usually did, reflected Sara, watching him closely, his eyes narrowed in concentration. 'Quite a few of the scientific journals have carried articles. . . . Wish I could get a story from this boy-friend of yours. But I shan't have time. Perhaps Joe'll send me out again.' He looked at her. 'Where is he now?' he asked, beckoning for the waiter again.

'I believe he has some business to see to.' She glanced

at her watch again. 'I must go, Graham. I might see you later.' But not if I see you first, she decided grimly. However, he asked what time she dined, saying he would join her and this boy-friend of hers.

'Well. . . .'

'Nothing serious, I suppose?'

'No, but——' She wanted to dine alone with John, but when she knew Graham was coming she did wonder how it could be contrived.

'Does this bloke know you're a journalist?'

She nodded her head.

'I mentioned it, yes.'

His pale blue eyes were a mask, as usual.

'Tell him what you'd been on?'

'No, it wouldn't have been of any interest to him,' she answered with a careless shrug of her shoulders.

'What's his name?'

'Parker—John Parker.'

'English, then?'

'That's right. There are lots of English working here in various capacities, and Americans and others.'

'You seem to have learned a lot—but didn't get the story.'

'Aren't you glad?' she could not help retorting, and he laughed as he replied,

'Of course. But I didn't expect you to. It was a crazy idea of Joe's, sending a woman. They might have got equal status, but nothing'll give them the strength and stamina of us men.'

She rose from her chair.

'I must be going——'

'Why?'

She flashed him a glowering look.

'You're a colleague,' she reminded him, 'not my boss!'

'Okay—sorry. How about tonight, though? If there's no lovey-dovey attached to this affair with Mr Parker the archaeologist, then neither of you will mind a third party at your dinner table.'

Sara drew a breath, but accepted the inevitable.

'We shall be dining at about half-past eight,' she said.

'Fine! It'll give me time to unpack a few things, and then to make a few phone calls.'

'Phone calls? You know people here?'

'I've a few contacts—did a bit of homework before I came, not like you who almost always muddles through—with some measure of success, I'll grant you——'

'Thanks—for nothing!' she flashed, looking down at him contemptuously. 'Who are these people you're intending to phone?'

'Never you mind! I just did a bit of homework, as I said. It struck me that there must be people here, in the capital, who have some kind of contact with this wild man of Borneo who's so damned elusive. For instance, he's not living up there without trading with the coast. All the tribes trade with the coast——'

'Not all,' she broke in, every nerve tight. She had known—oh, yes, she had known that Graham would have some clever method by which he could make a start at solving the mystery of the white man who lived in the jungle!

'All except the very remote, the Punans, for example, who live mainly on what they can find—well, most of them do.'

'You *have* done your homework,' she could not help saying, a tart edge to her voice.

'I like to have a background before I begin. What's the betting that I succeed where you've failed?'

For answer she swung away, his laugh ringing in her

ears as she went towards the arched doorway leading into the hotel lobby.

John was there already; she told him that Graham had just arrived, and that they were having dinner with him.

'I'd no alternative,' she said unhappily, seeing his frown. 'It's going to spoil our evening, I know, but what could I do when he asked if he could join us?'

'Nothing,' returned John soothingly, taking her arm and ushering her outside, into the gardens where he found a seat for them, beneath a clump of meranti trees. 'Now, tell me all about it. He must have caught an earlier connection from Singapore?'

'Yes, I suppose so; I didn't ask him. John,' she said apprehensively, 'I do feel that he's dangerous.'

'He's intending to chase a story, you mean?'

She nodded, her eyes shadowed.

'I know you're going to say I'm worrying unnecessarily, but I happen to know his ways, his stratagems, and you don't.' She went on to tell him everything that had been said and saw his brows knit together when she mentioned Graham's intention of contacting people here, in Kuching, who might know something about the white man. 'He's so expert at picking up clues, John,' she said finally.

'Well, let him get on with it. I doubt very much if he can glean anything here. The people who know me are the last who'll help him, aware as they are of my wish for privacy regarding my affairs.'

They talked a little longer, and when at length John felt she was in a happier frame of mind he took her for the walk around the town, returning after darkness had fallen and just allowing themselves enough time to change for dinner.

*

The restaurant was lit by candles only. The table reserved by John was secluded, tucked right away behind a screen of wrought-iron over which tumbled a lovely magenta bougainvillaea vine. The introduction had been made in the lounge, and now the three were at the table, each having been handed a menu.

Sara was uneasy. Knowing Graham so well, she was aware of excitement bubbling up inside him, and was not at all surprised when, the meal over, he asked John if he could speak to Sara privately. Her nerves tightened; she shook her head, but John spoke before she had time to do so.

'Of course,' he replied. 'I'm not Sara's keeper.'

She coloured but, meeting John's eyes, she realised that he wanted her to go with Graham . . . wanted her to discover the reason for his excitement! So John had seen it too. But suddenly she was remembering that sixth sense of his, that keen alertness and perception he had acquired through living for years in the jungle.

She went off with Graham, saying she would meet John later, in the garden under the meranti trees. Graham grinned, but that was all. No comment came from him; he was far too absorbed in his project to care about Sara and her activities.

'Guess what!' he burst out once they were in the lounge, away from anyone who might overhear. 'I've got my first clue! Our wild man of Borneo's here, in Kuching! What luck! You didn't even begin to go the right way about it, Sara——'

'He's . . . here, you s-say?' She hoped she was not as white as she felt, or that her heart was not thudding as loudly as it seemed to be. 'But how——?'

'Before I came I got in touch with a reporter friend who was here about two years ago, doing a job for the journal *Wild Life.* I asked him for contacts and he gave me the name and address of a fellow he became friendly with, a chap who's a voluntary worker on the Social Welfare Council here, in Kuching. He's a Malay—this social worker I'm talking about. I phoned him and he gave me my first clue. He saw—actually saw!—this wild man of Borneo in Kuching today! Coming out of a barber's shop in Ewe Hai Street. I raced along to the shop in a taxi, but it was closed and no amount of knocking brought the proprietor to the door. I'll be there tomorrow, though!' He stopped, bringing out a handkerchief to mop his brow. 'It's hellishly hot in here. Don't they have air-conditioning?'

Sara ignored that, making a tremendous effort to sound casual as she said,

'If there's nothing else, Graham, I'll be going.'

He grimaced.

'I suppose I've caught you on the raw over this. Sorry——'

'You're not at all sorry. Nor have you caught me on the raw, as you call it.' She took a couple of backward steps, half turning. 'I'll say goodnight, as I don't suppose I shall see you again until the morning.'

'Just a minute,' he said quickly as she took another step. 'Are you going to leave me on my own? Not very sociable, are you?'

'I expect you'll survive. It won't take you long to find someone to chat with in the bar.'

She went out into the darkness, hurrying away from the hotel to where the meranti trees made nebulous, uncanny shapes against a sky already becoming angry.

To her surprise John was not there. She called softly but received no response. It was evident that he was nowhere about, so she returned to the hotel. As she entered she was given a sealed envelope by the desk attendant and opening it she read,

'Sorry, dear, but I've been called away and won't be back till the early hours, so I'll say goodnight.' It was signed briefly, 'John.'

A flood of disappointment swept over her. Quite unreasonably she blamed Graham for taking her away from John, but the next she had switched her thoughts, wondering what could have taken John away so suddenly. He had received an urgent message, it would seem.

As there was nothing to be done about it, and as she had no intention of going back and joining Graham, she made her way to the lift, which took her to her room.

John was not in the restaurant when she went in for her breakfast, and another wave of dejection came over her as she sat down and picked up the menu. Graham was bound to come blustering up, she thought bitterly when, glancing towards the door, she saw him enter.

'Hello—good morning! Where's the boy-friend? Not an early riser, obviously.' He seemed immune to her icy silence as he grabbed a menu and immediately gave his order. Sara gave hers—a slice of toast and a cup of coffee.

'I'm not hungry,' she replied curtly when her companion asked what was wrong with her appetite.

'You look pale—no, fed-up——' He stopped and gave her his full attention. 'Something's troubling you,' he stated emphatically. 'Want to confide?'

She looked at him, her eyes flickering contemptuously.

'I wouldn't want to confide in you,' she retorted without any attempt at civility.

He merely shrugged, and when his breakfast arrived he tucked in and spoke only when he was ready to leave the table.

'See you!' He grinned contentedly and added, 'I'll have some interesting news for you when I see you at lunch time!' And without affording her an opportunity of answering he was gone.

She was at a loose end all the morning, expecting to see John, but if not, then to receive a message.

Graham's face was a study when, at a quarter to one, he bounced into the lounge where Sara was sitting with a drink, chatting to another guest—a man from Brunei who worked for an oil company—the same company as John's friend had worked for.

'Sara. . . .' Graham spoke softly and she felt an involuntary shiver pass along her spine. 'I want to have a little talk with you.' He looked at her companion insolently. 'You won't mind? Miss Chesworth's a colleague of mine and we have something important to discuss.'

Sara frowned and was about to intervene when the man rose, his face taut, and moved away to a far table without so much as an apology to Sara.

'You're—ignorant!' she snapped. 'Don't you ever use your manners?'

Graham sat down, his cold blue eyes never leaving her face.

'I can't make out whether or not you know,' he murmured almost to himself.

'Know—what?' Her throat felt constricted. She knew the answer to her question even before she asked it.

'Your Mr John Parker,' replied Graham slowly, 'is none other than the white man we're looking for.'

Silence. She knew it would give her away, but she was helpless to break it. She saw the movement of his sneering mouth as a thin smile touched it, and even the cold eyes seemed to have acquired some slight measure of expression.

'So your luck didn't desert you?' she managed, wishing with all her heart she could have seen John last night to warn him. It was too late now. Graham was hot on the trail and she was convinced that he would somehow manage to delve deep into John's secrets.

'I didn't expect it to.' His manner changed to one of puzzlement as he asked, 'Why didn't you try to get the story? Did you fall in love with the bloke?'

She felt that to talk any more without first consulting John might worsen matters—although at present she failed to see how they could be worsened. However, she intended to see John before committing herself in any way at all, and with this resolve firmly fixed she told Graham she had nothing to say to him and despite his hurried and persistent attempt to keep her, she turned on her heel and walked away.

Where could John be? The idea that he had decided to play safe and return to the *ulu* did cross her mind, only to be dismissed immediately, since she was convinced that no matter how dangerous his position was in the face of Graham's investigations, he would never leave without saying goodbye. No, there had been too much between them for that. He cared for her; she was sure of it. But of course he knew there could be no future for them, and he would have had to leave her anyway. But not like this, without one word of farewell. Where, then, had he got to? she asked herself again.

'Miss Chesworth!' She was about to take the lift up to her room when the voice from the reception desk halted her. 'A phone call for you. You can take it in your room.'

'Thank you,' she said, her pulse fluttering as she turned to the lift. It could only be John, she thought, waiting in a fever of impatience for the lift to come.

'Sara!' She was hearing her name a few minutes later, relief spreading over her in spite of her deep anxiety. 'I'm delayed for another few hours, but I hope to be with you for dinner.'

'Oh, John, I'm so glad to hear your voice! I've been in a fever of suspense because Graham's discovered——' She stopped as something went wrong with the line. It seemed dead. However, John's voice came over within a few seconds and it was clear that he had not heard her last words.

'I've tried to get you on the phone several times this morning, but there's been something wrong with the line. I've been told by the operator that I can have only three minutes——'

'Where are you?' Sara interrupted hastily.

'In——'

'I am sorry,' came another voice over the line, 'but your time is up.' The line went dead immediately. Sara replaced the receiver. Well, at least she had received a message, and knew John would be with her later in the day.

Deciding that it would do no good to sit around and brood, she made up her mind to do some shopping for souvenirs. This, she thought, would lessen the risk of bumping into Graham. But to her amazement she bumped into him the instant she emerged from her room . . . and he was coming from the direction of the room occupied by John!

Everything became clear in a flash. Knowing the unscrupulous methods which Graham could employ, she felt she should have anticipated this particular contemptible trick.

'Sara—' he began, when she interrupted him, lashing out with her tongue in a furious condemnation of his action in going into John's room.

'Was it not locked?' she demanded finally, her eyes smoulderingly fixed on his closed fist.

'It was locked,' answered Graham calmly, 'but often in hotels it's possible to get the key of someone else's room. Not nearly enough precautions are taken——'

'What have you learned?' demanded Sara furiously. 'You can be prosecuted for what you've done!'

'Hold on a bit, Sara!'

She looked at him, struck by the strangeness of his tone. He was grave, by no means gloating as she had half expected him to be.

'What have you learned?' she asked again, her legs suddenly weak, and a fluttering sensation in the pit of her stomach. Had he learned everything about John, and his past? Surely John would not bring private papers down here with him? And yet, thinking a little more about it, she supposed he might feel they were safer with him than in the hut.

Graham was speaking, asking her to go down to the lounge with him as he had a great deal to tell her.

'I'll just return the key,' he added casually when they were in the lift.

'How did you manage to get it?'

'From the desk clerk. He was a young Malay who'd just come on as a relief; he didn't know me by sight, nor, it seemed, did he know your friend John. I reckoned he wouldn't when I decided to ask for the key of number two hundred and two. He handed it over without question. They nearly always do; it's a wonder more hotel rooms aren't robbed.' The lift stopped and they got out, Graham going to the desk while Sara made her way to the lounge. It was deserted so she could have her choice of the several secluded corners. Graham joined her, asked if she was drinking. She shook her head impatiently, puzzled and intrigued by his manner. He ordered himself a whisky, his eyes expressionless as usual.

'Sara,' he began, slowly, hesitantly as if he were not sure of what words he would use. 'This fellow Parker . . . you knew he was the man you came out here to find, yet when you did find him you made no attempt to get the story. I asked if you were in love with him——'

'Let's cut out the irrelevancies,' she snapped, 'and get down to what's important!'

'Okay.' His drink arrived; he dug into his pocket for the money to pay for it, then lifted the glass to his lips. 'The story began about eight years ago,' he said. 'Just before you came to the *Sphere*. I was on it. Sir John Deverell, a surgeon who'd done some miracle operations, was struck off the register for making a serious mistake which caused the patient's death. His wife was working with him in the theatre, but nothing much was said about her at the time. Sir John admitted his guilt and disappeared. Nothing was known of his whereabouts. His wife divorced him and remarried.' He paused, deep in thought. 'That was the end of the story as far as it went. However, while you've been away another part of the same story broke—and I was on to it right away!' He was talking more loudly now, excited by his reflections. 'The wife was in a car accident and on her deathbed she admitted that it was she who had made the slip that killed the patient. Her husband shielded her—not only for her sake but for the sake of her mother, for whom Sir John seems to have had a deep affection, his own mother

having died when he was a child. In her confession the
wife admitted that at the time of the operation she was
in a temper, furious with her husband because he was
telling her what she must do—he was in charge of the op,
but she was performing it. She always hated the idea that
her husband was becoming famous while she stayed in
the background. Apparently, at the vital moment when
the slip was made, Sir John's attention had been called
for by the anaesthetist, who was checking the patient's
heartbeats. The slip was made and nothing could be
done. The man died.' Graham paused, noticing Sara's
white face, the convulsive movements of her mouth. 'Sir
John is of course cleared, and will be able to resume his
career.' Another pause and then, significantly, 'Are you
still mad at me for going and taking a look at his private
documents, for discovering that your boy-friend's not
only titled but that he's free to go back where he belongs?'
No answer and after a space he asked her how much she
had already known.

She hesitated, then told him everything. It was the
first time she had felt even the smallest degree of cordiality towards him, but his disclosure seemed to have
drugged her mind to everything except the vital fact that
the man she loved had done nothing wrong after all.

'So you actually met him in the jungle?' Graham's
voice was tinged with envy. 'He actually attended to your
injuries?'

'I've just said so.'

'And you fell in love with him.' It was a statement; his
excitement was high. Here was another part to the
fascinating serial, he was thinking. 'There'll be a
wedding! I'm on to the whole story of the romance!
Lord, what a scoop——!'

'Sir John,' she interrupted quiveringly, 'happens to be married already.'

'Married——?' He stared at her, a glitter of incomprehension in his eyes. 'Who to?'

Sara looked down at her hands, clasped tightly on her knee, aware that she ought not to have said anything about John being married. It would be a more sensational story than ever, the eminent surgeon marrying a Native girl, a dark-skinned savage from one of the most remote tribes of the Borneon jungle. She could imagine just how it would be treated by Graham, whose passion for the highly dramatic was known to every journalist on the *Sphere*, and to those on dozens of other newspapers besides.

'I'd rather not say, Graham,' was her lame and rather belated reply. 'I expect you'll be talking to John, and I expect he'll tell you what he thinks you ought to know— and nothing more.'

He grinned, saying confidently,

'He'll be so grateful for the information I'll be giving him that he'll fall over himself to give me the full story!'

'For once in your life,' she declared emphatically, 'your optimism's going to let you down.'

'You won't give me a clue to this wife of his?' he asked persistently.

'No,' she replied, 'I won't.'

The cold eyes were unfathomable.

'A mystery, eh? Why, if he has a wife, is he here with you, gadding about like a single man? Where is this wife? Was she with him in the jungle? You never mentioned her, Sara. . . .' There was something insidious in his tone, a sort of purring vibrancy that sent shivers running along Sara's spine. 'You know . . . I have a hunch.' The last word was spoken in his more usual noisy voice. 'My hunches are rarely wrong. . . .' His voice faded to silence as he saw her sudden change of expression. 'What——?'

'John!' she breathed, a smile fluttering. 'You're earlier than I expected.'

He had approached and was standing beside her chair, looking down into her pale face, a sort of contented expression in his eyes.

'Yes, I'm earlier than I thought.' He sat down, glancing at Graham. 'I have things to say to Sara,' he said abruptly. 'I'm taking her away.'

'But—Not yet . . . *Sir John*. I'd like to have a chat with you——'

'Undoubtedly,' broke in John smoothly. 'But as I don't happen to want to chat with you I'm afraid you're going to be disappointed.' The merest pause and then, 'Sir John? You've evidently been busy.'

A guffaw from Graham before he answered,

'It's my job to be busy when a great story's the end product. I——'

'Sara dear, come along. I've far more important matters to talk about than those which this fellow's concerned with.' With a proprietorial gesture he took hold of her hand and pulled her unresistingly to her feet. Her heart was light and she wondered why. For her conflicting thoughts kept reverting to Sri, his Native wife.

Ignoring Graham's protest, John ushered Sara towards the french window leading out to the gardens. In a quiet spot beneath the meranti trees he spoke to her, and the first thing he said was,

'I'm not married, Sara darling, so please take that look of sadness and despair from your lovely face.' And before she could utter the bewildered question that rose to her lips they were sealed by his kiss. 'My love,' he murmured, his mouth caressing her cheek, 'there's so much to explain—but first let me kiss you again.' A silence ensued, long and tender and, for Sara, filled with ecstasy as the blood raced through her veins. At last he held her from him, but no words were spoken even then, for he seemed too full to speak as he gazed into her eyes, taking his fill of their beauty. And in the end it was Sara who broke the silence, telling him everything that had transpired. He became grim when she mentioned Graham's going into his room and examining his private papers. Both he and the hotel manager would hear from him later, John promised, but said that for the present there were other things to think about.

He went on to explain that he had been called away by a friend in Sibu who had just returned after a month in England. He had expected John to be in the *ulu*, but his young Dyak houseboy had been able to tell him that he was in Kuching, at the hotel.

'It's the only friend, apart from my bank manager, who knows my true identity,' John went on. 'He'd read all about the affair in the English newspapers while he was over there,' he continued after saying that this friend had told him all that Graham had told Sara, about the accident in which his ex-wife was involved, and her subsequent confession which had cleared John's name. 'As you've had it all from Graham there's no need for me to go into details,' he continued. 'However, there was a little more to it. My wife happened to be having an affair with the man she later married, but at the time I had no idea it was going on.'

'No wonder you've been bitter, John!'

'It's all over now, sweet.'

'But there are lots of questions I want to ask.' She looked at him with a hint of diffidence, but he told her to 'fire away' and he would answer all her questions for her. 'First, of course, there's Sri——'

'Who is married to a Native boy who's had a very good education in Kuching. The two were married very young. He was taken away by his father to be educated while she was left. Makota became rather proud of his achievement, and somewhat contemptuous of his lovely young wife, Sri, who became my ward in a way although she did have parents. The *penghulu*, troubled by a possible break-up of the marriage, asked me to take her under my wing and do something about educating her. I did begin to teach her English, but she wasn't interested at first and even later she learned only a few odd words which weren't much good on their own. Then an emergency arose. Makota sent word that he wanted a divorce.'

'That was why Sri was crying?' interposed Sara when John paused, and he nodded, saying that it forced him to act.

'I needed no persuasion really, as I wanted to have a few days with you in Kuching.' He looked deeply into her eyes and digressed for a moment as he said that on several occasions he had thought about asking Sara to marry him, but as his name had been blackened he felt he could not do so. 'While I was in that sort of disgrace it was impossible to ask any woman to marry me——'

'*I'd* have married you, John!' she broke in eagerly, then stopped, appalled at what she had said. 'Oh, I didn't mean—er—I wasn't——'

'Proposing to me?' he said in some amusement. 'No, don't, my darling, for I assure you that *I* shall get round to making the proposal within the next few minutes.'

Sara coloured and they both laughed.

She said reflectively when she had recovered her composure,

'John, when you said the Press had written only the truth about you—you were lying. Why?'

'I was lying,' he admitted, but went on to explain that the Press *believed* they were printing the truth.

'Of course,' she returned. 'I see that now. But you suffered, you said.'

'I did. They tore me apart——' He broke off abruptly. 'Enough of that! What other questions do you want answering, my love?'

'Did you manage to put everything right for Sri?'

'Of course.' He smiled, saying he had digressed and forgot to return to the question of Sri's future. 'I told you you were right when you said you thought I'd been doing something for her. After I'd had my hair cut I took a taxi the short distance to the house where Makota is living at present. I wanted to find out if he loved her, and it seems that he does, because when I told him she was to be educated he was delighted and vowed at once that he definitely loved her and wanted her to come and live with him in Kuching. So that's another happy ending,' he added, and, drawing Sara to him, he bent and kissed her tenderly on the lips. 'Any more questions, darling?'

She thought of the Native girl, Luli, recalling how she had suspected there was an intimacy between her and John. But she could not voice the question, and in any case it was unimportant. It was probable that he had had more than one Native girl since coming to Sarawak and taking up the life of a Native, but it was none of her business. And it certainly was not as Joe had predicted— that once a man has had a Native girl he never wants an English one!

She thought, too, of what John had said about never

leaving the jungle, and this time she did ask a question.

'I did say that,' he agreed, 'and I meant it at the time. I still want to remain here, in Sarawak,' he went on to say, watching her expression intently to note if any changes took place. But she was serenely waiting for him to finish, which he did, with confidence, for he knew that if he wanted to go to the end of the world she would eagerly go with him. 'I can do good work in the hospital here, Sara. We can live in one of the bungalows you like so much. It's all very civilised down here, just as it is in any town. We shall of course live away from the town itself and I shall travel to the hospital every day.' He held her from him. 'I know that's suitable to you, so I won't ask you if it is.' Sara smiled and made no comment, and for the next few moments she was prevented from speaking anyway, caught as she was in the vortex of his passion when pain and pleasure mingled to send her pulses racing madly and her heart throbbing so violently that he felt it and brought up a tender hand, soothingly to caress it.

When at last his ardour had died down a little he looked at her and said,

'Any more questions, love?' Yes, she had just one, she returned, asking why he had told her he was married to Sri.

'Because I felt it would solve a few problems. You see, Sara, I knew you were falling in love with me and as I couldn't ask you to marry me—as I've just said, because my name was blackened—I decided to tell you I was married. I knew that would put you off, as it were.' Sara said nothing. She could see the logic in it but wished all the same that she had not been deceived into believing he was married, because then she would not have suffered so much heartache. He spoke again, saying with a trace of amusement in his tone,

'My turn for a question, dearest. And it's not "will you marry me", but can you manage to be ready in a week?'

'A—week!' she gasped. 'But my dress——'

'A week, my love,' he broke in imperiously. 'Good lord, how long does it take to buy a dress! Half an hour——'

'John,' she laughed, 'I'm not going to church in a sarong, you know!'

He laughed and her heart caught.

'I suppose,' he said with a resigned sigh, 'it'll have to be a week. I *was* intending to suggest we brought it forward.'

'A week. . . .' Why was she hesitating? It wasn't as if she did not know him well enough. No, perhaps it was because she knew him too well! A doctor he might be, but the years he had spent in the jungle had left a mark that would never be erased . . . the mark of the heathen, the savage. . . .

And as if to strengthen her conviction he suddenly crushed her to his iron-hard body and once again she was drawn into the whirlpool of his primitive passion.

She was breathless when at last he let her go.

'Oh. . . .'

'Oh—what?' His grey eyes were filled with tender amusement now as they gazed into her dark and dreamy ones, then he laughed as she lowered her lashes, trying to hide from him what he knew already.

'You took my breath away,' she said in answer to his brief enquiry.

'You liked it, though.' He tilted her chin so that she was forced to look at him. 'I believe you'll marry me in a week,' he said confidently.

She nodded, answering huskily,

'Yes, dearest John, I'll marry you in a week.'

His low laugh was triumphant.

'In spite of those misgivings you were having a few moments ago?'

'You're too perceptive!' she said pettishly, and received a little shake for her trouble.

'You've said that before, my child. It's something you've got to live with—that sixth sense I mentioned. The years in the jungle were bound to leave their mark,' he said, repeating what had been in her mind. His lips came down, meeting hers in a hard demanding kiss; his body was hawser-strong and possessive. Yes, there would always be something of the savage in him. Sara smiled to herself, for suddenly she knew she would not have it otherwise. He was her ideal, the one man in the whole world she had waited for, a man apart from all others, her dear, dear heathen!

'The next week,' her lover murmured close to her lips, 'is going to be the longest we've ever lived.'

She said nothing, but just relaxed in his arms, her slender yielding body pressed close to his, her mind lost in a dream as timeless as the jungle that had brought them together. . . .

The Mills & Boon Rose is the Rose of Romance

Every month there are ten new titles to choose from — ten new stories about people falling in love, people you want to read about, people in exciting, far away places. Choose Mills & Boon. It's your way of relaxing.

April's titles are:

PROMISE AT MIDNIGHT by *Lilian Peake*
Her job as pianist on a Mediterranean cruise liner should have been fun for Shona — but she had to cope with the unreasonable sarcasm and dislike of Marsh Faraday!

CALL OF THE HEATHEN by *Anne Hampson*
Obtaining a newspaper story from a white man who had 'gone native' in the remote jungle of Borneo was far from easy — and that was before Sara complicated matters by falling in love with him ...

DARLING DECEIVER by *Daphne Clair*
Carissa had been a silly, romantic teenager when she had had her first dramatic meeting with Cade Fernand. Now, after eight years, they had met again, and it was obvious that he still despised her ...

LAST APRIL FAIR by *Betty Neels*
Phyllida discovered that she didn't really want to marry Philip Mount when she met the kindly Pieter van Sittardt — but all Pieter could do was urge her to marry Philip ...

THE THAWING OF MARA by *Janet Dailey*
Mara hated all men — but would Sin Buchanan, with his constant needling and his accusations, melt the ice in her heart?

CLAWS OF A WILDCAT by *Sue Peters*
Margaret realised that she would have to control her love for the uncompromising Dominic Orr when he told her, 'I travel alone, I can't be bothered with encumbrances — however attractive.'

DECEIT OF A PAGAN by *Carole Mortimer*
When Templar's sister had a baby by Alex Marcose and then both she and Alex died, Templar took the child herself. But Alex's forbidding brother Leon didn't know all this ...

STORM CENTRE by *Charlotte Lamb*
Lauren's ex-husband had lost his memory and was asking for her, under the impression that she was still his wife. She had gone back to him — but how long could she stand the situation?

NIGHTINGALES by *Mary Burchell*
Amanda had a promising future as a serious singer — but she also needed money. Should she earn that money by using her talent by becoming a not-so-serious singer?

TIGER SKY by *Rose Elver*
Rescued from an awkward predicament by the masterful Luke van Meer, Selina knew that she could trust him implicitly. But could she trust herself?

Mills & Boon Classics

The very best of Mills & Boon
romances, brought back for those of
you who missed reading them
when they were first published.

in
April
we bring back the following four
great romantic titles.

CINDERELLA IN MINK
by Roberta Leigh
Nicola Rosten was used to the flattery and deference accorded
to a very wealthy woman. Yet Barnaby Grayson mistook her
for a down-and-out and set her to work in the kitchen!

MASTER OF SARAMANCA
by Mary Wibberley
Gavin Grant was arrogant and overbearing, thought Jane, and
she hadn't ever disliked anyone quite so much. Yet . . .

NO GENTLE POSSESSION
by Anne Mather
After seven years, Alexis Whitney was returning to Karen's
small town. It was possible that he might not even remember
her — but Karen hoped desperately that he did.

A SONG BEGINS
by Mary Burchell
When Anthea began her training with the celebrated operatic
conductor, Oscar Warrender, she felt her dreams were coming
true — but would she be tough enough to work under such an
exacting taskmaster?

If you have difficulty in obtaining any of these books through
your local paperback retailer, write to:

Mills & Boon Reader Service
P.O. Box 236, Thornton Road, Croydon, Surrey, CR9 3RU.

Masquerade
Historical Romances

Intrigue
excitement
romance

FOLLOW THE DRUM
by Judy Turner

To escape an arranged marriage, Barbara Campion fled
from home determined to find her soldier sweetheart.
Daringly disguised as a boy, she enlisted in the Rifle
Brigade and followed the drum through Belgium to
the Battle of Waterloo — under the command of the
fascinating Captain Alleyn . . .

STOLEN INHERITANCE
by Anne Madden

Deborah Wyngarde's journey to London with her
brother Philip, to claim their inheritance from the
newly-restored King Charles II, seemed wasted when
they were scorned as impostors. And Deborah had
meanwhile lost her heart to the Earl of Mulgarth —
whom even his sister declared to be a hardened rake!

Look out for these titles in your local paperback shop from
11th April 1980

Doctor Nurse Romances

and April's
stories of romantic relationships behind the scenes
of modern medical life are:

PICTURE OF A DOCTOR
by Lisa Cooper
Doctor Luke Garner obviously considered Virginia a
feckless, immoral artist, incapable of doing anything
worthwhile. Why should she mind so much?

NURSE MARIA
by Marion Collin
Nurse Maria's love for Steven Ransome put her whole
career in jeopardy. For Steven was her patient, and
'fraternisation' was strictly forbidden . . . .

The Mills & Boon Rose is the Rose of Romance

Look for the Mills & Boon Rose next month